UNRAVEL

UNRAVEL

BOOK 2 IN THE UN SERIES

KAILEY BRIGHT

Unravel

Book 2 in the UN Series

Content warning: Depression and suicidal themes

ISBN

979-8-9882306-0-1 *Paperback*

979-8-9882306-1-8 *Ebook*

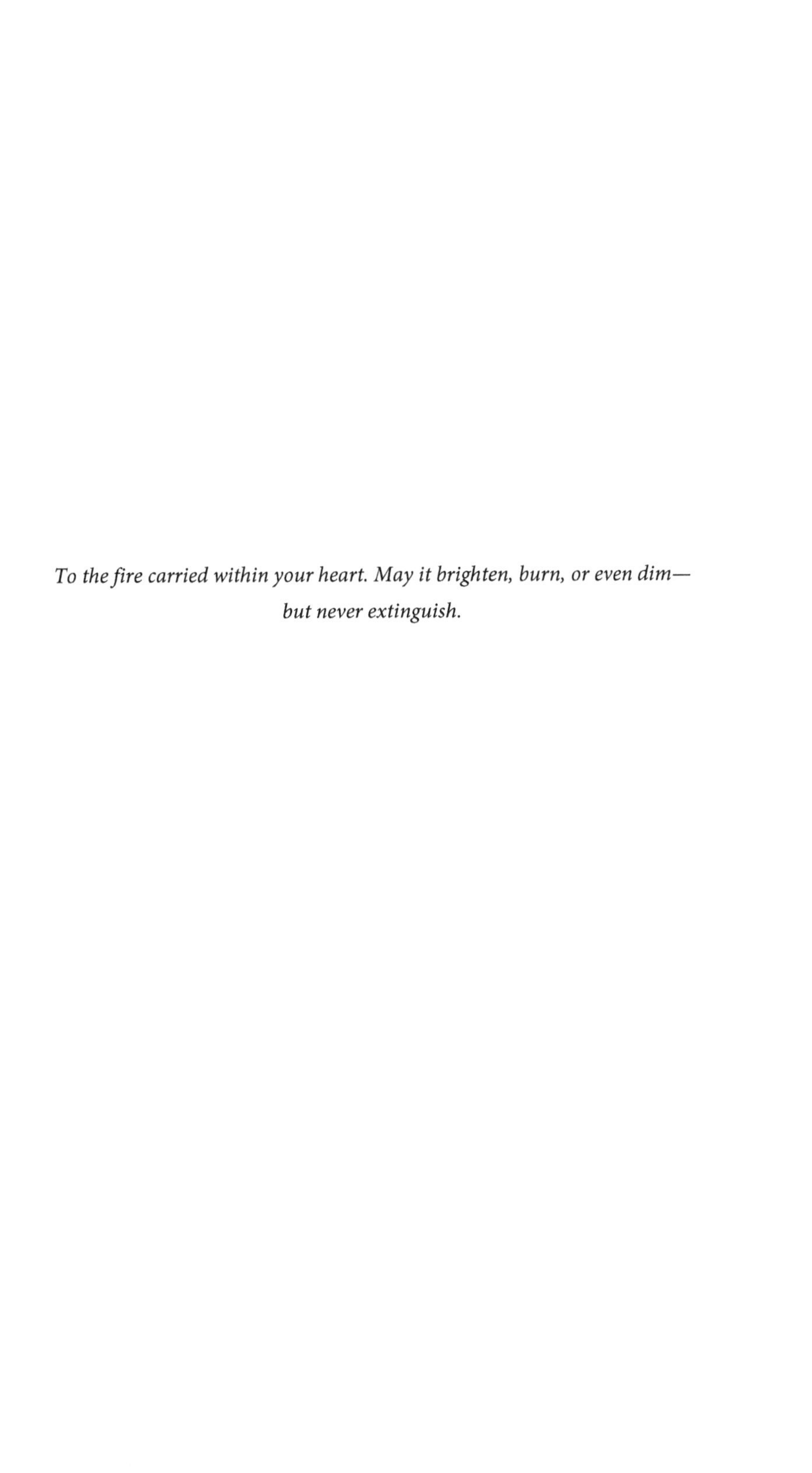

To the fire carried within your heart. May it brighten, burn, or even dim—
but never extinguish.

Contents

Author's Note

Dear Readers,

Have you decided how you feel about the rain? If you're impartial to a downpour, then I must express my deepest sorrow. If you despise rain with every fiber of your being, at least we can agree on our passion. And if you're not quite sure how you feel about the rain, I can't judge you.

Uncertainty brings an *UNRAVEL* in Book 2 of Nora's journey. As the Diviner gains more strength in his stolen Animus Gift and gains more support in his allies with the Unfortunates Nora swore to uplift, her unbreakable promise begins to wane.

And I must confess, dear reader, that I've done some unraveling myself.

While writing Book 1 during my Junior year of college, I was rigid with my schedule. For four months, I dedicated 13 hours to six classes, and dedicated the last 6 waking hours to my novel. Afterwards came the social media posts, the pre-sale campaign outreach, the post-campaign outreach, stressing over the cover design, revising, and so much more that would only exhaust this list further. As it turned out, repeating the first stage again wasn't as sustainable the second time around as I had hoped.

Instead, I surrendered two hours by falling asleep at midnight, cared for my body by waking up an hour earlier for the gym, treated myself to quality time alongside a lovely pumkin, and consumed every M&M on campus while creating a website from scratch. Telling my roommates I finished a log-in system and the first chapter on the same day was only funny the first time.

Even though I regained some agency over my routine, I still felt pulled in all directions and ripped at the seams. I still needed to write my book and finish assignments on top of these newfound habits. And much like Nora and the others at Galdor Academy, the outside world around me continued to spiral and spin.

It's hard to be brave despite fear when you feel so powerless against forces out of your control. After all, what could one person do to mitigate large-scale conflicts? In late February and beyond, I kept asking myself that very same question.

As I watched what happened in Ukraine, I kept looking off at the cloudy sky and at the sun setting in the west. I wanted to stay in that peace for just a little bit longer. Forever, if I had my way. Although it was improbable that global war would focus on rural South Carolina, the fear of impermanence haunted my thoughts. I feared everything I knew would unravel and morph and disappear. I feared my world would reflect Iridion's, so writing *UNRAVEL* became a necessity.

The same fear gripped me while my boyfriend and I drove through the backroads in early summer when the greenery was at its brightest. We passed trees gutted from lots, their thinner limbs, leaves, and other undesired remains left discarded in the dirt. My boyfriend explained that the owners sold the trees but had no reason to clear the land. Worries of global warming, deforestation, and forest fires drew my mouth into a despondent line.

We drove in silence for another mile stretch, both contemplating the same worry. But there was something alleviating about our collective worry beyond our car. Like those large-scale conflicts were manageable because we could brave our fears together. But I'm getting ahead of myself for Book 3.

This book is ultimately for anyone who wants to make great change, either in themselves or in their community, but holds uncertainty in their heart. *UNRAVEL* asks: how can one person make a difference? That question, as Nora will discover, can only be answered when you're stripped down to your bare essence.

Stay ambitious.

From one Unfortunate to another,
Kailey Bright

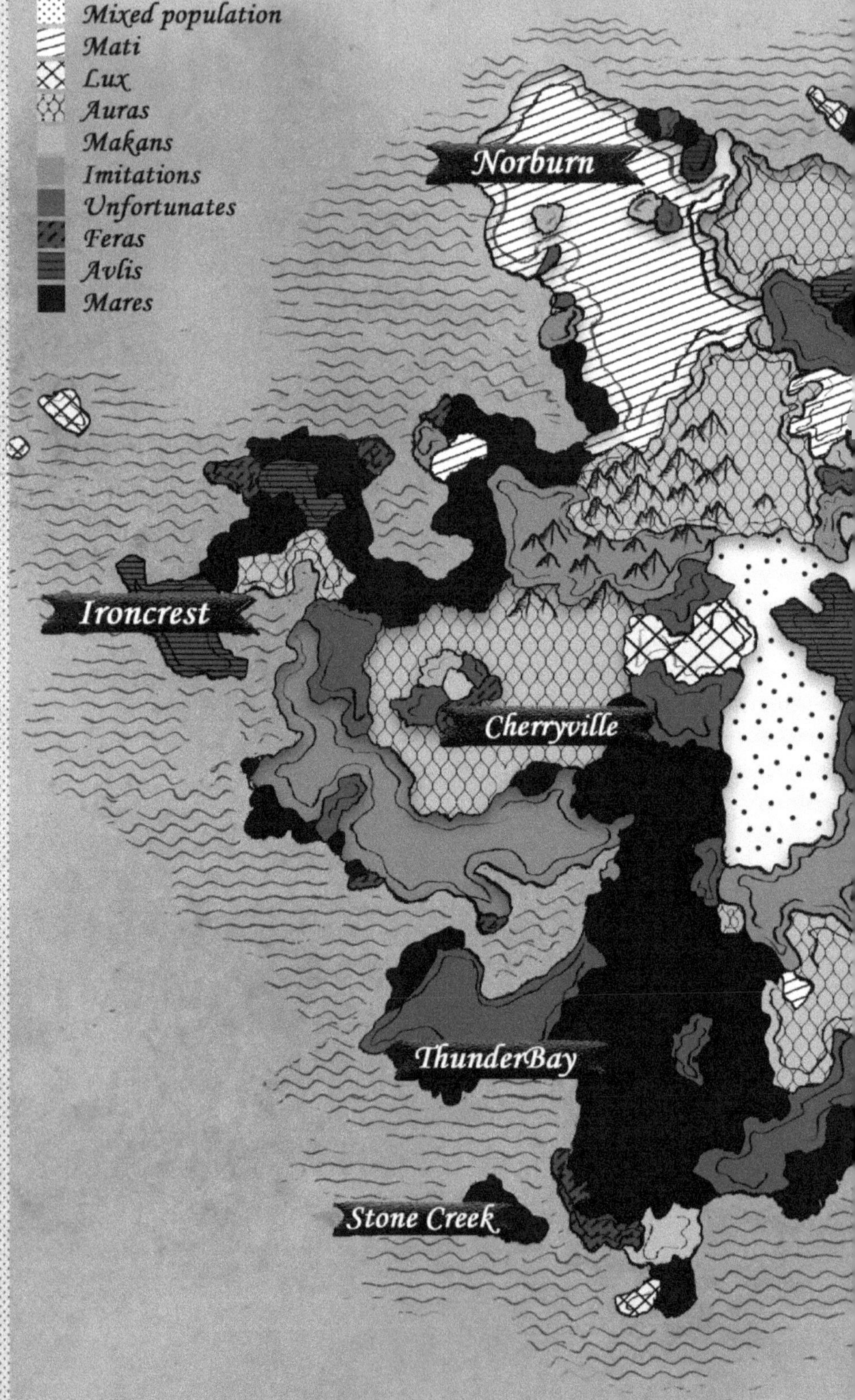

Mixed population
Mati
Lux
Auras
Makans
Imitations
Unfortunates
Feras
Avlis
Mares
Norburn
Ironcrest
Cherryville
ThunderBay
Stone Creek

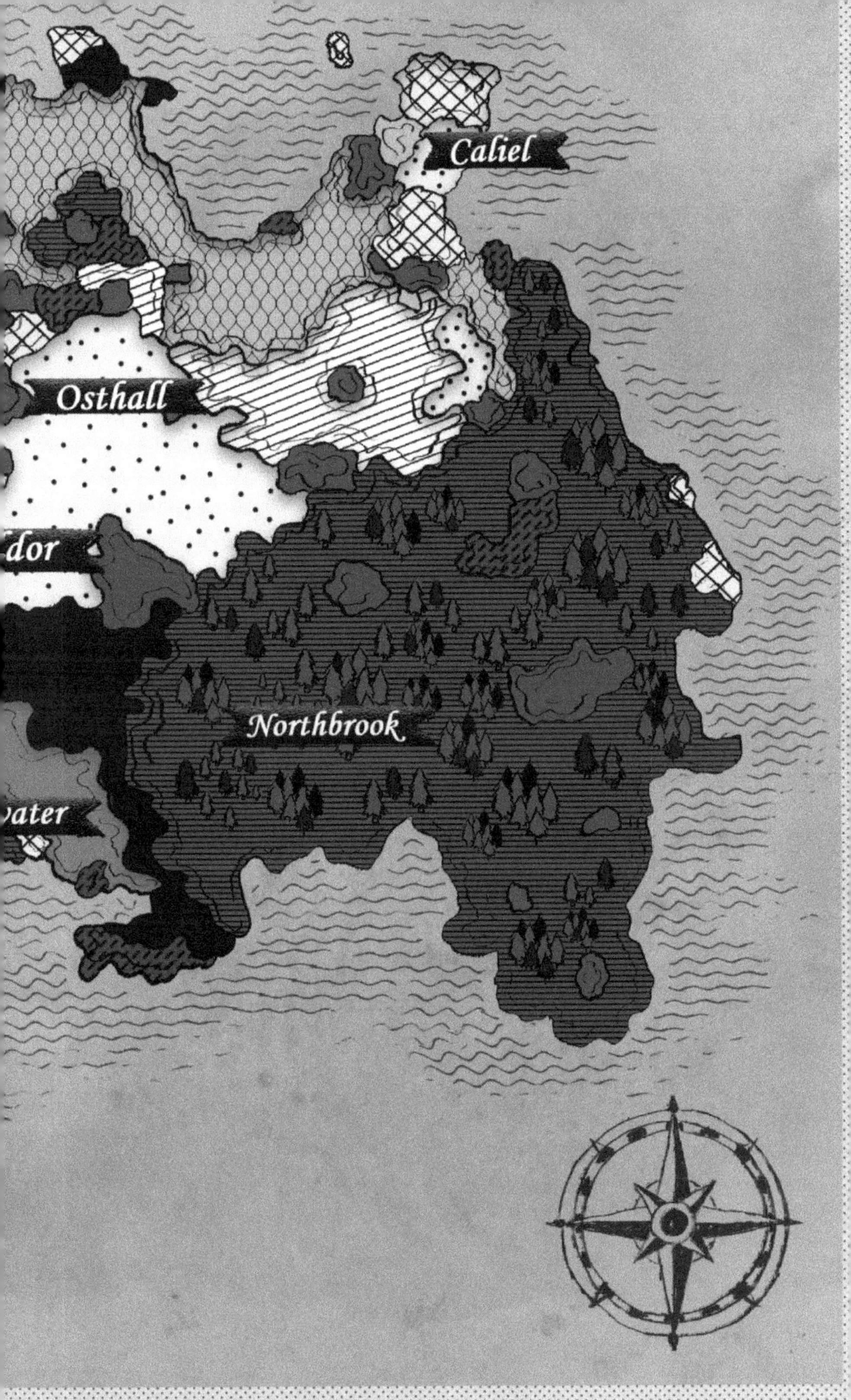

Caliel
Osthall
dor
Northbrook
ater

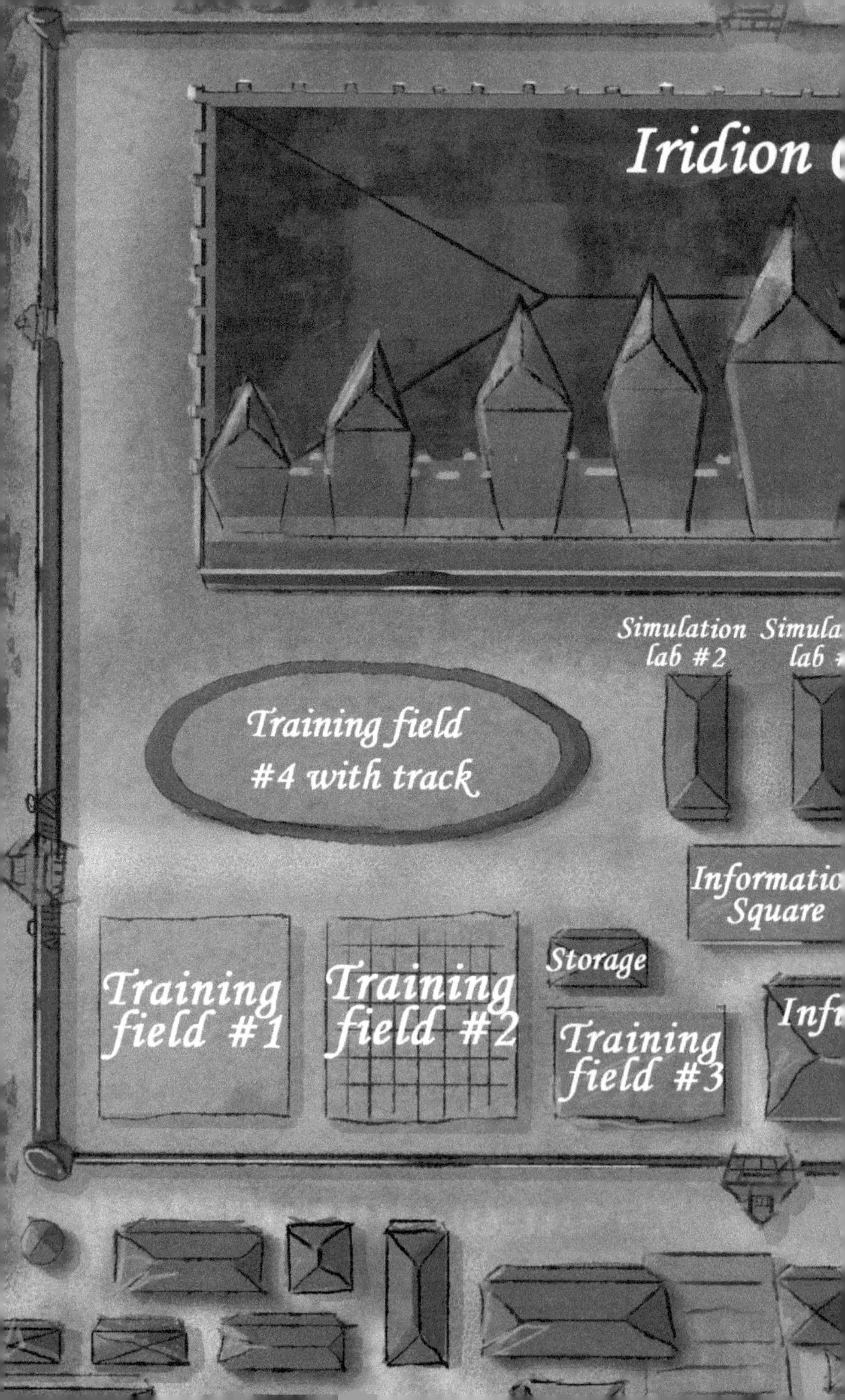

Iridion
Simulation lab #2
Simula lab #
Training field #4 with track
Informatio Square
Storage
Infr
Training field #1
Training field #2
Training field #3

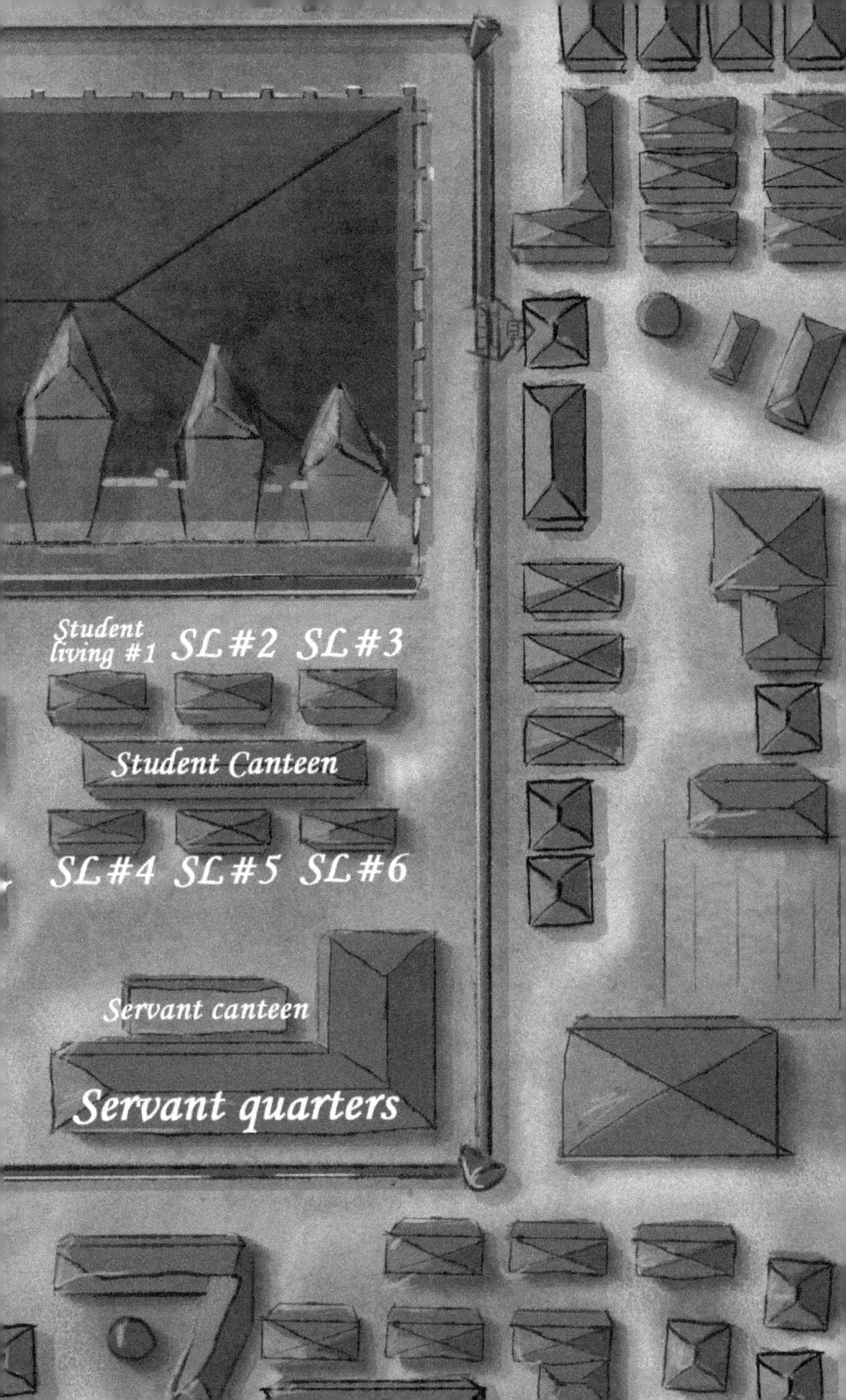

Student living #1
SL #2
SL #3
Student Canteen
SL #4
SL #5
SL #6
Servant canteen
Servant quarters

CHAPTER ONE

Above My Reach

—

My one consistent solace back into reality splintered apart further and further each morning. The rough textured ceiling meant I was at Galdor Academy. Meant I was safely tucked into bed and surrounded by friends shuffling awake. But the shelter above our heads rotted away—piece by piece, day by day—above my reach.

My eyes still heavy from slumber and my mind still clouded

with his image, red hair caught my peripheral like an all too familiar armband.

I slowly shifted my attention from the ceiling to Fern. She sat down at the edge of my bed and reached out, "Let's get up, Nora."

Her fingers found my wrists and tugged; I pulled myself into a sitting position.

Even though we moved over to the second-year dorm building, the layout was almost exact and no one changed bed arrangements.

Kai examined the scarred burns along Leo's arm at his bedside. Persephone hovered like she did every morning as Kai spoke through his entire process for her.

"The infection is almost gone, and you're healing well. Try moving your thumb."

After several heartbeats of intense concentration, all five of Leo's fingers flexed in sharp movements. Persephone sighed in relief.

Kai smiled, "Even better. Keep doing that for a minute."

Skylar watched the check-up on her bed across the room, tying her blonde strands back into a braid. Standing nearby when Leo commanded lightning at the Determination, Skylar now bore thin zigzag markings along her fingers and forearm. Almost like the signature trademark of a Mati Gift that the twins adorned naturally, though she would hate such a comment dared said out-loud. She pulled long sleeves over her arms.

Molly tucked herself into the corner wall. Downcasted by the Diviner's hand, Molly Montgomery no longer resembled the vicious Gifted who tormented me throughout my servitude. Assigned to the castle during the Determination, she saw no action to prove herself worthy of staying at Galdor.

Her parents hadn't written back to any of her queries about coming home. Iridion's second Unfortunate soldier was not a title she wanted for herself either, so she remained as paralyzed as her situation.

I frowned. Cassius's presence prickled up my spine like the chill of an overcast as I thought of him. Squeezing Fern's hand to stay tethered, she squeezed back.

We remained in that silence until a knock jumpstarted my nerves.

"I got it," Kai declared.

Kai opening the door revealed a servant with her non-branded hand folding over the other. She lowered her head in silence and stepped out of the way for Princess Maya to pass through. Everyone did the same.

Did you sleep late again? Cassius's voice echoed through my mind, taunting me in my waking thoughts too.

I stumbled out of bed and shakily rummaged through my drawer, ignoring him as best I could.

The princess watched me struggle with her gloved hands folded against her chest.

"I don't like being kept waiting."

"I'm sorry, Your Highness." I bowed in front of her properly.

Princess Maya inhaled. "I need you to be consistent in your personal royal guard duties, Nora."

Consistent. I glanced at the splintering ceiling.

"Yes, ma'am."

Kai found his chance to speak as I scrambled.

"Your Highness." He stood in front of her. "I think the entire class would like to know how Mr. Harris is recovering. Do you know when we can start training again?"

The princess shook her head. "Mr. Harris is still in recovery and cannot provide for his country as the 1st Senior Royal Crest Knight let alone as your instructor. He sends his deepest regards."

"Permission to change classes then, ma'am."

We all halted, surprised by the immediacy in his voice.

Princess Maya challenged him. "Reasoning?"

"I—" Kai shakily replied. "I need to succeed at any possible opportunity, ma'am. Second years are required to start their Emergency Response training, and I'm limited to gift technique and history lessons instead. Please, ma'am. I need to progress."

We all glanced about, waiting for the princess's reply.

"I'll have it so that you start ERS training at the infirmary this week. With the state of our country, they could use every assistance feasible." As Kai's shoulders relaxed, the princess lifted an authoritative index finger. "But you will remain in this class and maintain all other courses already assigned to you by Mr. Harris and your new instructor, Mr. Winters."

None of our eyes could get bigger than Kai's at the mention of the 2nd Senior Royal Crest Knight.

"Will that help you progress, Mr. Lancer?" she asked.

The Mare nodded as non-frantically as possible and bowed his head. "Absolutely, Your Highness."

I adjusted my collar. "Ready, ma'am."

"Before you're alone with her, ma'am—" Skylar punched me square in the face before I could recoil. I yelled and held my cheek. Every fiber in my being had to hold back from retaliating. This wasn't the first time; Skylar was just getting better at surprise attacks.

Seeing my features unchanged, Skylar nodded her head in approval with a satisfied grin that suggested she enjoyed this method of confirmation. "Okay, she's not Ebony Nique today."

Princess Maya's servant pushed herself further behind the doorframe as Princess Maya herself held a wide-eyed expression. She struggled to respond in an appreciative voice.

"Thank you, Miss Stanton. For securing my safety. I'm glad to see Nora...as herself."

Skylar pressed her hand on my shoulder, pulling me in her direction and throwing me off balance. "You're Nora for *now*. I want a rematch."

"Tell that to Leo." I pushed her hand away and walked towards Princess Maya. "He's the one who saved you from Ebony with that lightning strike."

Skylar's face darkened at that comment. Huffing, she held her finger up like she was about to correct me when the words never left her mouth.

Satisfied with her reaction, I followed the princess out to the corridor, down the stairs, and into the castle.

We walked in silence, careful not to brush up against each other.

"I'm sorry about Mercy," Princess Maya finally said.

I glanced to the Unfortunate behind us. Her blonde hair was wrapped tightly in a bun and hidden partially by the bandana sometimes servants wore while they were cleaning. It was an Unfortunate I didn't recognize, but perhaps she was just another shapeless being that blended into the walls—those perfectly sculpted marble ones so cold and pristine to the touch.

"Mercy, ma'am?" I asked.

"The Waltons thought to give me a present. The new Head of Household thought that in his brother's failure to bring the Diviner to justice, it would be appropriate to give me one of his Unfortunates."

Poor, poor Mercy. She could be you, you know—nothing more than a gift to the one you serve. My hair pulled back behind my ear. *Or you could always give yourself to me.*

I jolted, unsheathing my sword to the empty air.

Princess Maya and Mercy recoiled. "Nora?"

Several heartbeats passed without incident.

I sheathed my weapon, "Sorry, ma'am."

Regardless of what Gift he stole, his Makan power remained with him.

Each blink brought the dark blue color of the world back to me.

He vanished within that blink, within that loud clash of thunder, at the Determination. The last time I saw him. *Really* saw him as both Animus and Makan. As both the powerless prince who comforted me in his dance and the power-hungry messiah who caught me in his web.

In between seeing him then and hearing him now, I couldn't decipher if he was in my mind or here in the hallway—invisible and staring directly at me.

I blinked again and realized we entered the princess' private study. Dazed by the sudden shift in surroundings, I watched as Mercy cleared off and organized the desk. The princess already leaned back in a chair, tapping her gloved fingers on the desk as the servant laid out a notebook and pens. What...? When did we...?

Slowly sitting in the cushioned chair, I thanked Mercy as she finished.

Princess Maya sat upright, taking off the crown atop her head and gently placing it at the corner of the table.

There was something about taking off her crown that straightened my back in alarm; how the princess before me let out a deep sigh with a gentle hand against her neck in a long-awaited stretch with a face almost barren like she had taken off her identity and had become something of equal ground to me.

Maya noticed as she reached for a book, her eyes filled with a sudden alarm. "What's wrong? Do you need help getting started?"

My eyes fluttered with a ting of embarrassment. "No, ma'am."

She started reading; I turned back to my work. Fiddling with the nearest pencil, I watched it twirl in my unbranded hand. The wood grooves rubbed against my thumb, reminding me that I was indeed awake.

I opened the notebook, passing by my first 100 scribbles and landing on the latest pages organized by repeated N's, O's, R's, and A's. I recognized my name separated out across several pages, but it had been years since I actually wrote it. Starting back from scratch.

The princess periodically checked as I filled a sheet with uppercase A's followed by a sheet with lowercase a's followed by a sheet with both uppercase A's and lowercase a's.

"Now write each letter together to form your name." Princess Maya gestured to a new page where she had written, "Hello, my name is" with enough space for me to practice.

I stared at the blank space, my heart sinking at the reminder of my inadequacy. The pencil pressed irregularly into the paper, so meticulously slow that the lines drew jagged and awkward.

Princess Maya noticed my frown. "Keep going."

I did, repeating my name and then the phrase and then new sentences related to myself in different rhythmic timing and pencil strokes.

As I filled the page, a light knock interrupted our lesson.

Mercy opened the door, and Minister Gabriel stood in the doorway. I hated how quickly I looked away, fearful that he would somehow see Cassius reflected back behind my eyes.

Princess Maya's face scrunched as she noticed his presence. Her voice lowered, removed from any encouragement she had before.

"Is it time already, minister?"

***

Staring into the mirror, I waved my branded hand to remember I was in fact looking at myself.

"This is unnecessary, ma'am." I dared to stick my nose up to avoid my reflection. "If Mercy does not have to appear like a Gifted, I don't see why I must."

The two servants behind me stopped styling my hair.

"Mercy is not a Galdor student," the princess countered matter-of-factly. She waved to the two servant girls. "Get her along in her dress now, please."

One servant girl retrieved a garment wrapped in plastic—light-yellow fabric that would have looked better on you, Valerie. "I thought this was a funeral, ma'am."

"The dress isn't bright or flashy." Princess Maya stopped writing to show her fingers adorned with light yellow jewels. "Look, we'll be matching."

"Put me in red so I can look like the AGM member the minister expects me to be," I refuted. Both servants froze, hovering over the box filled with bracelets.

"Don't dare joke about that," Princess Maya snapped. "If you want permission to speak freely, you must do so instead of acting like a child." She turned away from me to keep writing, but she hovered over the paper.

I paused, realizing from that stern expression how far I pushed her. No doubt my inner thoughts were slipping out more than I ever intended. It was a trait I recognized in myself around Mr. Harris. And now Cassius was weaving through my words.

What could I tell the princess that she didn't already know? The death of any royal family member demanded the entire kingdom to mourn. Despite Cassius's declaration to the world at the Determination Arena, Princess Maya still wanted a public event in honor of her mother and father. She pressed on despite my hesitations, too.

We compromised on a small funeral publicly recorded, but the few permitted to the funeral were vital to the government system. And Cassius knew where we would be in just a few hours because of his connection to me.

I already gave you my word, Nora. Cassius read my thoughts but didn't mend my fears. *She shall give her speech to the world uninterrupted.*

I watched Princess Maya tap her pencil with a scrunched, concentrated face. I could tell her right now. I stepped closer to her. She would stop the funeral. And she'd be safe. And—

And you'd break all trust and credibility in her eyes, Cassius warned. *Minister Gabriel is finding any reason to label you an AGM ally. Can you bear that? For her to look at you with the same disgust?*

My mouth wired shut as Princess Maya noticed my stare in the mirror and turned toward me.

"Nora?"

I rubbed my hand along my arm. I found an excuse quickly, "Would you like assistance, ma'am? With your speech, I mean?"

"Please." Princess Maya waved me forward.

Continuing to switch between reality and my thoughts, I blinked from chatting in the office to apprehensive silence in the car.

I attended a few funerals in my lifetime. If something happened to any Montgomery relative or close friend, my strict responsibility was to make sure the House was as stress-free as possible.

Unfortunate funerals were more common and held on Sundays when servants could attend on their one day off under the 5th Unfortunate Law of Servitude. I couldn't afford a proper funeral for you, but I pulled all sorts of strings to give one to Sylvia Douglas once she was removed from the Galdor Academy flagpole.

The question *"why?"* had been the common outcry since the idea was proposed. My volition stayed imprinted along my subconscious: The government needed to show some respect to its citizens, for reassurance that Iridion still had morals.

They asked *why?* Because Sylvia Douglas was misguided and killed and put on display before my very eyes—before my own Unfortunate soul. Because she was a girl examined alongside me during the Choosing Ceremony. Because she was chosen by Gifteds, found a violent escape, and died for her freedom. Because if I hadn't kept my promise, I could be buried beside her, too.

A tug pulled on my yellow dress, and I looked at the Gifted choosing me for servitude.

Mercy stepped closer to me instead.

"Is everything okay?" Princess Maya came into focus, a concerned look covering her face. "You completely froze."

Looking around, I noticed the outdoors. Amidst the grey and clouded sky, another droplet splattered harshly against my cheek.

"It's raining," was all I could muster.

"Yes, I do believe it is." The princess straightened out her dress as she spoke. "Well, come along now. We must get to the summit before the funeral commences."

But my nerves didn't connect with my body. Rendered useless like I was controlled again by Mr. Harris or by the Diviner.

"It's raining," I repeated in a low whisper.

Before Princess Maya could speak again, Mercy lightly pulled me forward.

We arrived at the summit, no doubt the work of an Avlis. It uprooted the royal family and guards onto a platform that allowed them to overlook an empty space—where a mourning crowd of Gifted Houses and their Unfortunate servants would be if this was a proper funeral—if I had stopped the Diviner before the Determination.

The grey clouds moved and twisted above.

Still gripping my arm, Mercy assisted me upward. Minister Gabriel latched onto the princess, and Isaac Winters pushed back cameras eager to capture and record.

I turned my neck towards the servant to express my gratitude, but my lips remained still. As more raindrops became a soft rain, Mercy opened an umbrella and shaded us from the oncoming storm.

A Royal Crest Knight nearby leaned towards Princess Maya. "Request to have the Mares clear the perimeter of any rainfall."

"Let the Divine share his remorse for our loss, Your Highness," the minister urged.

The two stood there waiting for the princess's response

"Have one of your Mares shield me while I give my speech," she said. "If any camera crew needs a Mare, lend them one to protect their lens."

The two men nodded their heads and backed away. The rain continued to strengthen.

Black spots dotted my vision as several cameras flashed. A reporter pressed into my side. Mercy's grip on the umbrella fumbled.

"Any comments from the first Unfortunate soldier?" one asked, pressing her microphone forward.

Another did the same with the lines, "Do you feel personally responsible for the Diviner's attacks on the kingdom?"

Mercy quickly obscured her face. The lens adjusted and focused on the scene—all at once clicking and buzzing into place. Minister Gabriel made his entrance.

"Ladies and gentlemen," he spoke loudly in a dignified, commanding voice. His big brown eyes brought the cameramen to attention. "I give myself to the people, as the Divine has given so much to us. Let me answer any and all questions you have."

The media did not resist as the minister detailed his future political hopes and promises against the Anti-Gifteds Movement. More restrictions. More laws. More violence.

Gifteds never learned.

Cassius's nose brushed against my cheek as he whispered in my ear. *No one wants to kill the minister more than me, but you can kill him for me, Nora.*

My branded hand throbbed as I tried to find my sword underneath fabric. Greeted by empty rain, I awkwardly brushed my dress instead. Thankfully, only Mercy was paying any attention to me.

Cameras adjusted and focused on Princess Maya as she took her place at the very top of the summit. Her words rang out, starting low and cautious as she addressed her people.

"Today, we honor the memory of not just a mother and father but a king and queen—"

Cassius passed by my shoulder; my chest clenched until I noticed how his form blurred like watercolor in the rain. Haunting but not physically present. Like the tear above my head, every day was a new reminder of his growing strength.

Glancing about, no one else reacted in a way that suggested they could see him too. Their eyes remained on Princess Maya but mine remained on him.

"—our rulers of Iridion."

He moved effortlessly in the empty space in front of me. His left hand was lifted while the other remained in an L shape away from his body, as though he danced with a missing partner.

"But this tragedy doesn't come from an honorable place. The rift that separates Gifteds and Unfortunates has always plagued our kingdom, and its only proven to deepen and manifest into something more sinister."

Minister Gabriel stood proudly next to the future queen, his Lux Gift useless to seeing what was right in front of him. Cassius spun his missing partner and brought her back to him as Princess Maya continued her speech, guided by my input.

"But by the Divine, we must find a way to bridge that rift— to find peace in each other's open palms instead of violence in each other's closed fists. Is that not what the Great Book tells us? That thou shall hast no power when we defile the Gift granted to us?"

Contentment warmed Cassius's smile. My chest burned at the sight. I remembered when all anxiety washed away in his embrace.

"I fear Caliel will reign judgement if we maintain this

dangerous course without direction."

Cassius pointed his feet towards me.

"Only when we unite—"

He extended his body in an arch and outstretched his hand.

"—can we stop this impending unravel."

CHAPTER TWO

Eighth Law of Servitude

——

We walked to the senior circle meeting room in deathly silence, lost in our own thoughts.

Unravel, I thought.

The word burned its way through my scarred hand and gnawed at my heart. I glanced at Princess Maya next to me, her stride less commanding and her posture bent forward. I didn't want to attend this meeting either.

Every new piece of information given to me was also given to Cassius and the Anti-Gifteds Movement. And it was a futile effort to weasel my way out of Princess Maya's gloved hand. I offered Cassius a bargain.

With whatever you're about to learn, I started, *I need information too.*

His voice was incredibly calm, *Ask away.*

Your bracelet. Its glassy smooth exterior still felt cold against the nap of my neck when he kissed me before the Determination. Before his grand reveal to the world. *Is that how many Gifts you have?*

However many I want to carry.

So there were more. I didn't think he would tell me the exact number of stolen Gifts in his grasp.

How does a Makan possess such an ability? I asked.

I learned in Norburn. From a teacher. A king in his own right.

Split between my thoughts and the living world, I noticed we were halfway down the hall.

What did he teach you?

How to see Gifts.

We neared a corner; Mercy stepped in front of Princess Maya to check for clearance.

Walking back to her original position behind the princess, we turned left.

Cassius continued, *How to see them blossom and swirl and illuminate a person into a bright light.*

I glanced again at Princess Maya as she rubbed her fingernails.

Is that how you see everyone?

No.

We passed a servant who clung silently to the walls.

Unfortunates are hollow, Cassius clarified.

She bowed. Mercy bowed back.

Void of any light.

Is that how you see me? I asked.

A pause. *No.*

No? Damn, we were close. I didn't have enough time to press.

Is that how you knew Prince Henry is an Animus? I asked instead.

Yes.

The meeting room stared from the end of the hallway.

And Mr. Harris? I wondered.

Halfway there.

I had my suspicions. I knew he wasn't a Fera from the light he omitted, but when I saw Prince Henry for the first time, I finally understood when they shared a purple hue.

I knew that deep purple hue well. It blinded the stadium when Cassius took Mr. Harris's Gift for his own. Two Royal Crest Knights straightened their posture on each side of the meeting room door.

I only had time for one more question, *How do you take Gifts?*

Cassius recited to me, *If you can see it with the mind of your heart, and feel it in the depths of your soul, then you will hold it in your hands.*

The doors swung open to the senior circle meeting room.

His end of the bargain was fulfilled. Now to unwillingly uphold mine.

The meeting room stretched further from its sheer emptiness. Only two Gifteds were present.

Minister Gabriel stood closer to King Daltus's seat at the front of the table, and Isaac Winters took his place across from the minister where Mr. Harris typically stood.

Princess Maya trudged past the misshaped carving where the table met her poisonous touch. She teetered directly in front of but not daring to sit down in her father's throne.

"Today's discussion is in regard to successor," the princess's words started out mumbled. "We need an official and definitive person in power if we're going to bring Iridion back to its feet. Since we are in a bit of a bind, all suggestions are welcome."

"The regional head ministers and I had a productive

meeting earlier this week," Minister Gabriel jumped in first, "and we all agree that as Head Minister for the Church of Iridion and Spiritual Advisor to the reigning sovereign, it would be in the country's best interest to appoint me as regent while Mr. Peter Harris is...indisposed."

"Regent?" A bad taste eroded in my mouth as I spoke. I looked over to Princess Maya, uncertain of its exact meaning but understanding that Minister Gabriel was up to no good.

Isaac responded with a factual tone I couldn't match. "Perhaps you need to examine the monarchy laws a little closer, minister. No minister, yourself included, can become heir or even a legitimate member of the royal family."

"I do not desire either of those titles," assured Minister Gabriel.

He side-glanced in my direction. "We must act accordingly if the young Prince Henry is indeed an Animus as the Unfortunate claims."

I stood taller, shoulders back. "I'm telling the truth. The Diviner—"

"Cassius," Princess Maya interjected.

I forced his name outward, "*Cassius* told me that he was going to take Prince Henry's Animus Gift after taking Mr. Harris's."

"Yes, and we're supposed to believe that Mr. Harris was an Animus all this time too? When he himself is not a member of the royal family?" the minister pressed.

I still didn't have an answer for that, and Cassius remained silent in my mind.

"I speak the truth, minister. He..." I swallowed hard, "He used Mr. Harris's Gift against me."

Princess Maya folded her hands. "I believe my Unfortunate representative, minister. Until proven otherwise, Prince

Henry is now the heir assumptive."

She latched onto that idea ever since I first told her a few weeks back, right before she was released from the infirmary.

Minister Gabriel noticed too and took advantage. "Then you will agree that our 1st Senior Royal Crest Knight is unfit to act as regent until Prince Henry is of age. I suggest that the responsibility goes to—"

Isaac Winters.

"Isaac Winters." His name fell from my lips before I understood what that meant. I repeated Cassius's words, "as the 2nd Senior Royal Crest Knight."

The disbelief on Minister Gabriel's face almost brought a smile onto mine. He couldn't use ignorance against me here.

The minister recovered, turning toward Princess Maya. "With all due respect, ma'am, he became the 2nd Senior member a few weeks ago. He is unfit to be regent." He gestured to himself, "I have years above him serving under your father."

"But the law clearly states—"

"The law clearly states that I cannot become *heir*," the minister corrected me. "No rules prohibit me from being regent until either Mr. Harris or Prince Henry are capable of leading instead. Your Highness, this is the best decision for our country. Iridion needs its religious leader now more than ever to unite them."

I narrowed my eyes. "United against Unfortunates, you mean."

"United against threats to *His* people." The minister raised his nose toward the Divine. "I don't expect you to understand what that means."

"I don't expect you to understand either, minister."

A chill ran through the room and frosted the curtain edges. Isaac kept his arms crossed and expression hardened. "Your arguing is getting us nowhere. I will fulfill the requirements of my station if that is what Our Highness wants."

Silence. We all stared at Princess Maya who stared back with conflicted eyes.

I tilted my head. "If you didn't believe me, would you become queen?"

Her blue eyes pierced through me.

"Yes," Minister Gabriel answered for her.

She turned toward him but kept her mouth wired shut.

"Then if these are truly trying times, then you can remain the heir assumptive," I suggested, "or even regent for a time if that makes you more comfortable. No one outside of this circle knows what Prince Henry is, and you've been trained to become the heir for your entire life. Why are we considering anyone else?"

Princess Maya's lips quivered, "I—"

"Your Highness—" Minister Gabriel acted quickly but I cut him off.

"You want to stop this unravel as much as I do," I stepped forward. "What is your hesitation?"

"As your father's advisor—"

Princess Maya halted him with her hand. Eyes closed, she said, "As King Daltus's advisor, you shall then act as *my* advisor." Her face scrunched, "If the council votes majority, I will assume the role of regent until this crisis is over and Mr. Harris can take over in my place."

She looked out to the two council members present.

Grasping at straws, I thought. *But why?*

She called out the vote. There wasn't anyone else alive to do so. "If you favor Princess Maya assuming the role of regent for the time specified, please raise your hand."

Isaac Winters raised his hand.

"Nora," she glanced at me, "you get to vote too."

I raised my hand. Minister Gabriel huffed.

Princess Maya sighed, her crown slipping forward as she exhaled.

Every failure weighs on her incompetence now, said Cassius.

"It is done," the princess breathed.

"Then as your spiritual advisor, may I propose a new Unfortunate Law of Servitude?"

The minister's go-to move. I waited for Princess Maya's pushback.

"What do you propose, minister?"

Shocked, I snapped my attention to the princess who kept eye-contact with Minister Gabriel.

"It would be as temporary as your new position, I assure you ma'am. A mandatory curfew. We must stop the AGM from expanding and plotting."

"What would this new law entail?"

My eyebrows ruffled. She couldn't possibly be considering—

"Any Unfortunate servant out past ten o'clock without their Gifted owner will be brought to prison as a suspect."

No.

"Which prisons?"

This couldn't be happening.

"All that are close to their Gifted House."

Stop.

The princess contemplated this new law. "This proposed ULS law appears reasonable. I shall grant your request so long as I oversee the matter personally. Your hand is often more violent than necessary, minister."

"I act only in the Divine's will."

Her lips twitched in a small hint of irritation. She puffed

out her chest and tried to imitate her father's neutral stare.

"If that is all, you are dismissed. Mr. Winters, I would like you to assist the minister in drafting a reasonable use of force and prison room. Nora, you may stay behind."

The minister opened his mouth to object, but one look from Princess Maya shut him down. He and Isaac Winters left together.

As the doors audibly closed, Princess Maya slouched as she sighed again, looking past the ceiling.

"How did this happen?" her voice cracked; tears dampened and disintegrated on her face.

Mercy drew closer, thanks to years of consoling Gifteds within her Unfortunate instinct. My feet started to lean forward, but her deal with Minister Gabriel rooted me in place and separated me from her.

She allowed the monster to speak. Allowed him to create a new ULS law. I suddenly couldn't be outside without Molly present. Even though Mr. Harris brought me to Galdor, my legal status was not altered. I was still property of the Montgomery House. I still belonged to Gifteds.

Did that mean nothing to her?

Princess Maya didn't notice. She wiped her face, her voice filled with sudden urgency. "I need to leave."

"Leave?" Alarm heightened my voice.

"Where would you like to go, ma'am?" Mercy didn't miss a beat, clasping her hands together. Attentive. The best servant the princess could ask for.

"I don't know. I just need to leave the castle. I can't—" Her glassy blue eyes caught mine. "I need to reach my people before I become their queen."

You don't believe her, Cassius noticed.

My stare lingered, trying to piece together why the princess wanted to escape. No, I didn't believe her reasoning. Not completely. Seconds ago still haunted me, too. Where was this sudden need coming from?

Mercy continued, "Summer's coming up, ma'am. Have you considered Northbrook and the Flower Festival?"

"Northbrook," the princess glanced to the floor. A smile brushed her lips as an idea formed. She looked back at us. "Yes, that's good. I suggest we start packing."

"Packing?" I couldn't help but repeat her in bewilderment.

Neither were concerned. Neither were fazed. What could I possibly say that would revert the princess's actions now? I had to at least try.

"Maya," I reached forward to grab her attention and not her poisonous touch.

I wanted to ask about her leniency with Minister Gabriel, but water continued to pool into her eyes. Her face twitched, struggling to push away a fearful expression.

A seriousness hardened my voice. "Running away isn't going to solve anything."

Princess Maya looked away as the fear broke through. She frantically walked in circles around the meeting room. "I thought I would have…more *time* and in better circumstances. I'm not running away. I'm simply leaving. Immediately."

"Maya."

"Immediately," she pressed. "And that's an order."

INTERLUDE 1

"Promise me, Nora."

My attention deviated from the swaying grass as Valerie wrapped an arm securely around my smaller frame. The smell of chocolate chips enveloped my senses from the lodge—the home we talked about for each other. With each other.

"I thought I already had," I smiled, looking out at the bright blue coloring of the world. Not a cloud in sight. I inhaled slowly, the muscles along my spine instinctively relaxing.

Valerie leaned closer and rested her chin on my shoulder, leaning towards my neck. "Promise me again."

"What for?" I laughed. My fingers wrapped around her arm as the sky sank into a deep navy color. "We escaped together."

I turned towards her face, but Cassius returned my gaze, his expression somber.

"We almost did."

Gasping, I unlatched from his hold and stepped back. "Where's Valerie?"

Cassius extended into a polite bow and offered his hand; the same gesture every time. "You can keep your dream if you dance with me."

I will never stand with you. I told him so at the Determination Arena after he asked to dance with me then: after he commanded the Anti-Gifteds Movement, after he stole Mr. Harris's Gift and became an Animus, after he first overtook control of my senses, and after he declared to the world that he was the Diviner.

His expression softened to disappointment as his lips pouted. His eyes flickered downward, and his outstretched arm retreated. My resolve faltered for a heartbeat as my fingers fiddled with my dress, but my heart was known to betray me before.

A sword appeared in each of our hands. He expected my answer like clockwork; he knew my answer before I responded. How many more nights would he ask that impossible question?

I readied an offensive stance as Cassius inhaled.

"Begin."

He lunged at me; my breath hitched. Metal screeched as our weapons collided. My arms shook violently as I fumbled changing to a defensive stance.

Cassius looked down. "Remember the ox ward." He lightly kicked my left foot with his, directing my toes straight at him. I adjusted, the movement clunky like I forgot how to use my feet.

We locked eyes. "Align the blade with your face."

I aligned on instinct. Even now, he still taught me how to be a better swordsman. And even now, I obeyed. Who else was going to teach me?

"Now get out."

As I hesitated, Cassius repeated himself. "Now get out."

I pressed forward. He nodded, slowly pushing away from me.

I twisted my wrist to separate our weapons. Free in hand, my sword moved in a small circular motion.

But Cassius blocked my attack with his own circle parry, catching the tip and deflecting my blade. I jumped back and added distance before he could strike me.

Cassius halted and examined my new stance. Right foot forward meant I was in plow ward stance. I steadied the sword closer to my knees.

He attacked again. Cassius lunged; his sword propelled downward. Frantically, I swung before he could slice through my shoulder.

I threw his sword to my right; his body twisted to his left. An opening.

I raised the sword above my head.

But Cassius shifted back squarely in front of me, his sword held out horizontally. He blocked, jolting his arm up as we clashed.

Sharp iron bounced straight for my face. Stunned, I left myself completely defenseless.

Grabbing my shoulder, Cassius forced me closer and drove the sword into my torso. A light gasp escaped my mouth, the sudden shock coupled with my spliced nerves too overpowering to scream. My organs rubbed against steel; my body folded and slipped closer to the hilt.

In between shaky breaths against my shallow ones, Cassius ripped the sword away. Blood pounded in my ears and out of my chest as I fell to the ground.

Cassius looked down at me with sympathetic eyes. He dropped his sword, hands shaking and dripping red.

He collapsed beside me, lifting the upper half of my body so I could rest on him. I tried screaming but wheezes strained from my gritted teeth.

As I slept, he killed me often. Fresh and unrelenting, the pain never eased. I needed to wake up—escape the fire spreading through my body—but he remained in my sight.

His lips shaped into a tight 'o'. I could only hear him clearly in my mind—shushing me. Comforting me.

The consequences of my failure hurt him, too. Why, I couldn't decipher. Pain wrestled with any clear thoughts. Reminded me that I needed to get better. If I couldn't beat him in my dream, what chance did I have when reality came?

At least for now he could give me a kindness I could never give you.

Darkness developed my sight in longer takes as my blinks slowed. A raindrop wetted my cheek. Or was he crying? My eyelids remained shut.

His hands gently pushed hair away from my face. *We'll try again tomorrow.*

CHAPTER THREE

Plastic-Wrapped Escape

Eyes wide, reality came back to me with each unwavering heartbeat. Heat enveloped my body, and paralysis forced my gaze upward. I was at Galdor Academy. My friends slept around me. The ceiling splintered further apart.

I continued to look up even as the train slowly drifted to a halt into Northbrook, Iridion. The town was at the heart of the country's dense forestry, far away enough from Galdor to appease Princess Maya and close enough to Galdor to ease my mind.

We didn't use the official royal trainline specifically tailored to Princess Maya's needs as a Nox. There were too many chances for the AGM to know our exact location and strike—they could already know considering my connection with Cassius, but I didn't dare share that fact.

Instead, Mercy and I planned for our transportation at the very front of the train, so if Princess Maya did manage to destroy the train car from the inside out, the engine would erode before citizens did. We straight-laced precautions.

Draped head to toe, the Nox's skin remained hidden. Silicon lined the walls for extra security, and we all wore synthetic-laced clothing to help repel any accidental contact.

The doors opened, and I caught a glimpse of the impending Flower Festival. A delicate entanglement of vines and flowers now lined each train car.

We transferred the princess to a designated vehicle also lined with silicon on the inside. Mercy and I accompanied her accordingly while the rest of my teammates piled into the other vehicle, and Royal Crest Knights trailed us, too.

We arrived at an empty stretch of woods and proceeded by foot. The air cooled my skin from the overlaying canopy of trees. Light seeped and danced through the lush green leaves as the breeze rattled them.

"Come on, come on, come on!" Fern twirled and swung her baggage.

My shoes sank into soft moss. Exposed tree roots appeared like a network of veins.

Princess Maya fidgeted with her clothes. One slip and she could devastate an entire ecosystem. Why Mercy suggested here and why the princess had agreed was beyond me.

"Are you okay, princess?" I asked.

She inhaled a breath, her voice quick to avoid any hesitation, "Yes, I'm fine, thank you."

Fern caught me before I could press the princess further, spinning me around with a giggle. "Oh, my Divine, you get to meet my mom and Delilah and my trees! Oh! I get to see my trees!"

Fern let go and continued to twirl onward by herself. I watched her dance, how she appeared so completely oblivious in the middle of her hometown, in the middle of all the chaos festering within Iridion. So unhindered and unbothered. Like herself again.

"Mom!" Fern called to an approaching plump and built woman who shared the same red hair and a younger woman in a simple green dress standing beside her. Even from the distance, I could see where her mom's leg ended and the metal began.

The two embraced. Closer now, I could see her prosthetic better. Cylinder-shaped, the metal rod narrowed into a sharp point instead of a foot.

"Your Highness," she and the servant bowed.

Princess Maya nodded politely. "Ms. Fairaway. We're so thankful to be here. I hope it's not much of an inconvenience."

"Of course not, ma'am," the Avlis waved dismissively. "My home is wrapped and secured as requested."

Because she also refused the house specially made for her Gift. Reaching her people couldn't possibly warrant standing on a knife's edge. And yet, here we were.

"These are your teammates, baby sprouts?" Ms. Fairaway prompted. Her eyes trained on me and her hand was shaking mine before I understood what was happening. "You must be the Unfortunate student."

She maintained eye contact with a warm smile I couldn't interpret as deceiving. I glanced to the servant receiving a warm welcome from Fern. "Does that bother you, ma'am?"

"Not at all," assured Ms. Fairaway.

She moved on to Kai without explaining herself. So affirmed in her statement, I knew she was genuine. But the *why* still burned at the back of my mind.

Once she went through the line of Gifteds, Ms. Fairaway clapped her hands reflective of her daughter's usual excitement and led us further into the forest.

I focused on the Unfortunate in front of us, walking in stride with Ms. Fairaway. Another shapeless girl that blended in with her background.

As my mind and feet wandered, we finally halted.

"We're here!" Fern cheered.

Trees continued to stretch in every direction. We looked around cluelessly.

The Avlis rolled her eyes with a smile and pointed upwards.

We craned our necks to the sky. A web of wooden and roped bridges zig-zagged between the large trees, and nested in those thick branches were homes and huts that varied in size and shape and design. Small patches of light came in through the canopy from the absence of leaves, illuminating the area around us.

Bands of large wooden steps spiraled on several of the trees where women marked with a branded U climbed up and down.

Fern squealed, jumping and waving at those above. Ms. Fairaway encouraged us closer; the ground beneath our feet rumbled softly before breaking apart and uprooting into the air.

As we stepped onto the wooden bridge, Ms. Fairaway waved her hand downward and the platform returned to the earth.

Something crawled its way through my hair; I jolted at the thought of Cassius but it soon passed as small white petals ruffled through my fingers. It was just Fern.

Relief overtook my nerves until the panels creaked. I kept my eyes forward.

We treaded onward, arriving to a wooden house built into a tree. Split into two separate pieces, wooden stairs along the tree trunk connected the houses in thick, enclosing vines.

Heavy branches wrapped around the base of the houses to keep everything in place. Blooming flowers and moss decorated the exterior, brightening the home in a vibrancy of reds, yellows, blues, and purples.

We watched our step entering the bottom floor house. Wooden floors remained glossy and clean underneath a sheet of silicon that moved and crinkled as we walked. Family photos suffocated behind plastic wrap, obscured by a thin film.

"Amelia, have three of your girls settle our esteemed guests on the second floor, and then prepare a lunch for all of us if you haven't started already," instructed Ms. Fairaway.

The Unfortunate nodded quickly and charged down the hall as we waited at the door.

Your girls, I thought. From her accompaniment and fast-timing, Amelia must be the head servant of at least three other Unfortunates. How many others did Ms. Fairaway own?

As quickly as Amelia left, three Unfortunate women as promised (all around the same age as me) stepped forward in uniform long sleeve black dresses, their fingers exposed and eager to relieve our bags. But when the Unfortunates caught sight of my casual attire mismatched with my branded skin, they froze and hesitated.

"Would you like me to take your bag?" one of the closer and braver ones finally asked in a conditioned, polite tone.

A deep shame seeped and festered inside my chest at the request. "Oh no," I shook her head and pulled my luggage closer to my chest. "I got it, thank you."

The three girls nodded and quickly moved down the hall, luggage in tow. Their whispers caught my ears. *Did you see her? She looks so much smaller in person. Could she...?*

"Hey, Mom?" Fern called, breaking me away from the gossip.

As we followed her into the entertainment room, I looked around for Princess Maya. The Nox could tear through this house if she tripped, if a tear or hole exposed wood paneling, if one piece was left uncovered. Here, plastic overlaid a metal floor and the couch lined with a clear, tight sheet. The lamps stood dull and the shelves remained dormant. I looked around for any security breaches.

Fern leaned into the doorframe. "Where's Poppy? I didn't see her when I came in. Is she in the kitchen?"

Ms. Fairaway didn't look at her child, "Poppy is no longer bound to the Fairaway House."

"You gave her away? I knew she was a little difficult, but—"

"I didn't give her away," Ms. Fairaway cut her daughter off with the mother voice that meant this discussion was over.

Several heartbeats passed in silence.

Fern's confused expression tightened into one of excitement. "Delilah!" she twirled and grabbed at the air.

"You weren't supposed to know!" A smaller girl appeared out of thin air, thrashing for her release. I stiffened a gasp at the sight of a Makan.

The two laughed. "It's not my fault you're loud." Fern plopped her back down.

I recalled a Delilah in a previous conversation and noted that this younger girl had to be Fern's sister. From her size and disposition, I estimated that she was twelve years old.

Her irritated expression softened as the two hugged.

"Nora!" Fern gestured me over, "This is Delilah."

Fern squeezed her sister harder. She flickered from visible to invisible and back again. I gritted my teeth to stop from flinching. Her Gift reminded me too much of Cassius.

Delilah looked at me with a deadpan expression. "You're the Unfortunate soldier I've heard about in the news, right?

Can I see your sword?"

"*Delilah*," Ms. Fairaway warned.

But the younger didn't listen, disappearing within a blink of an eye. My back bristled as quick footsteps approached. Reappearing next to my hip, Delilah tried unsheathing my sword from its holster.

"Mom says I should learn how to use metal weapons soon. What alloy do you use?"

I grabbed her hand and pushed the hilt down, my knuckles whitening from so fearfully determined to keep my sword still.

"Delilah!" Ms. Fairaway put her hands on her hips. The metal floor moved by the scan of Ms. Fairaway's eyes. Her Makan daughter moved with it and away from me.

Her face scrunched, ready to fiercely disagree with her mother. "It's fine, ma'am," I blurted. "No harm done."

Ms. Fairaway eased, "Right. Well, let's not all just stand here. Come into the living room and get comfortable."

She gestured us forward; I continued to dart my eyes about, determined to find a spot unprotected.

Princess Maya must have noticed, too. She watched the others move away from her.

"Would you like to leave, ma'am?" I intentionally chose a double meaning.

"Would you like to freshen up in your room, ma'am?" Mercy asked in comparison.

A small stretch of my lips indicated my frustration. We needed to get back to Galdor as soon as possible.

"That would be nice," the princess addressed her servant and then addressed Ms. Fairaway patiently waiting on us. "I shall take a moment to freshen up. Where are my quarters?"

"Amelia," Ms. Fairaway called.

Amelia appeared behind everyone like a shadow

transformed from the wall. She was excellent at her job.

As we turned to leave, I heard Fern say, "Hey Delilah, how about we look through the Flower Festival decorations upstairs? I want to see Nora in a butterfly outfit."

"The Unfortunate?" Delilah questioned.

Butterfly outfit? I thought with the same disbelief.

I could already imagine the sheepish grin lightening Fern's face.

***

Amelia led us up to the second section of the house, completely silent and face forward.

The layout to the second floor was similar to the first. The kitchen and entertainment areas were replaced with rooms. We arrived at the furthest room from the exit. If Princess Maya did accidentally use her Gift, everyone else would have time to escape.

As Amelia opened the door, its silicon coating made an undignified sound.

Mercy bowed and side stepped to allow the princess and I to enter first.

Amelia remained outside the threshold. "If there is anything else you might need, please ask." She nodded and then she was gone.

Mercy closed the door behind us, struggling against the snag of plastic around the lock. But I paid attention to the princess instead as she slowly walked around the room. The space was about the same size as her study—much smaller than her accommodations at the house tailored to her.

"How are you settling in, Your Highness?" My voice was genuine and on a knife's edge.

"I'm doing as well as I can," she replied, tracing her gloved fingers along the wooden chair in front of a dresser. Her smile widened into an excited grin, "It's been so long since I've been to a *forest*. Look at me! I'm in a forest!"

I watched her glide haphazardly around the silicone protected room, how she appeared so completely oblivious surrounded by wilderness, in the middle of all the chaos festering within Iridion. So unhinged and grief ridden. I didn't want to ruin her enthusiasm, but...

"May I speak to you alone, ma'am?"

She paused; her smile faded. "Granted."

Mercy nodded, but the door didn't shut all the way on the other side.

"Why are we here now instead of Galdor getting ready for your coronation?" I murmured, "and why did you permit Minister Gabriel's new ULS law?"

The princess swallowed hard. "I can certainly answer the second part."

I wanted to ask about the first—to understand how she planned to stop the Diviner so far away from influence. But the quick twiddle of her thumbs didn't stop so I didn't press.

"I know that my brother would easily call me careless in my duties for allowing the minister to speak—let alone take action. And I'm not vapid. I know you feel the same way."

Dread crept into my heart, freezing me in place like an Animus Gift. I didn't like how she was right.

"But with so few of us left, the kingdom needs some stability among its highest members. It's better to remain in good faith with the minister. So many look up to him, and we need people to keep good faith with our government. Minister Gabriel can keep his curfew idea under strict Divine jurisdiction."

She pressed a gloved hand to her chest. "As the direct link to the Divine and His greatest strength, Minister Gabriel's law is under *my* jurisdiction. I have and always will choose nonviolent means as the solution to Iridion's problems, and I can make sure he does the same. Besides, you can surely agree that this is a passive way to stop the Anti-Gifteds Movement from growing or organizing."

We stared at each other for several heartbeats. On the surface, Minister Gabriel's request did make sense. But this affected all Unfortunate servants, and even if he managed to capture AGM members instead of regular civilians, what was stopping him from harming them in prison? What was stopping those on the fence between apathy and action to finally brandish a red armband?

"What would you do if the minister *does* act with violence?"

When she didn't respond, I continued, "What if I stayed out past curfew without Molly?"

"Nora," she dragged my name out dismissively.

"The Unfortunate Laws of Servitude clearly state that a Gifted is permitted to discipline their servants how they please, and resisting can result in death. *I* can be put to death at any moment."

"Stop that."

"But I can! The Montgomerys still own me, and Minister Gabriel has enough power to do what he wills without permission."

"Nora! *Restrain yourself.*"

All other words ceased as anger seared the princess's face.

Princess Maya lost the expression with a sigh, putting one of her hands against the forearm of the other in a nervous, awkward gesture. We sat in silence as the princess twiddled with the rings on her fingers.

"I need Minister Gabriel to remain agreeable," she explained. "He can't be replaced. The kingdom requires a spiritual advisor, and the regional ministers he holds court with do not have the same expertise. Not to mention how many Gifteds support him. He can actually *reach* my people."

She kept using that phrase: reaching her people. Is this why she was risking everything leaving the castle? For some semblance of being who she always wanted to be? Like an Unfortunate?

"When can I see Mr. Harris?" I asked instead, knowing quite well that this was not the time. He needed to come back. At this rate, Minister Gabriel would unravel the entire country before Cassius ever tried to take it over again.

Princess Maya sighed deeply in frustration. "Nora, you know he refuses to see anyone while he's recovering."

It was my turn to sigh.

A light knock on the door interrupted us before I could press further. "Yes?" asked the princess.

Mercy opened the door, "Pardon the intrusion, ma'am. The Fairaways are requesting Nora's presence. When shall she be available?"

Princess Maya stared at me and stopped the conversation there. "She can be available now."

CHAPTER FOUR

A Purple Butterfly

Fairaway servants clipped at my skin and tightened my corset with worn and wrapped fingers. Mine were bruised too with a different, more dignified purpose. But to say that also meant to discredit what these girls were doing. They were just as resilient, as resourceful, and as obedient as any soldier.

Truly, the only difference between me and them was our sitting arrangement.

"How is that, ma'am?" the Unfortunate hesitated and stuttered saying "ma'am" once she was complete, brushing down my short dress.

"You don't have to call me that."

The Unfortunate kept her head lowered and hands folded. "You look beautiful, ma'am. Would you like to go on to makeup now?"

Sighting Amelia staring with narrowed eyes across the room, I narrowed mine back. Was she upset that I was an Unfortunate, pampered by other Unfortunates? Or was she a strict head servant that made sure that all the other Unfortunate girls maintained poise and etiquette?

Perhaps a little of both. I don't know how I would react if someone else was in my place. How would I feel if I had to dress another Unfortunate for a festival I could not enjoy? If I had to tend to her like a Gifted guest?

Easy. I would hate her.

"Sure," I spoke slowly.

The Montgomerys didn't designate a head servant between me and Valerie. We were equals, catching each other's mistakes and brushing each other's sides to remind ourselves that we weren't alone. We had each other.

"Why does Persephone get to be the flower?" Skylar's cynical voice broke out through the room. Arms crossed and eyes narrowed like a child, she stared at Persephone who sat patiently with a Fairaway servant.

Delilah's face turned to a deep red at the Aura's comment, "It's because Persephone is the prettiest out of all of you."

Skylar fell silent, and the young Makan vanished from sight to go find a dress piece in the other room. It took everything in my power not to laugh. I've never seen someone shut her down so quickly. Leo could certainly take notes.

The Fairaway servant continued to place sunflowers in Persephone's hair, brandishing a smile that wasn't in the performed, polite way. No, there it was—her eyes squinted as her mouth opened. A laugh escaped so suddenly and so quickly, the Unfortunate tried desperately to hide her lips with her hand. Persephone must have said something funny.

The sudden action deviated Amelia's hostile stare from me to the laughing Fairaway servant, and her eyes quickly lost their twinkle. The illusion that this wasn't work had vanished just as quickly as Delilah had.

My servant turned my chair towards the wall, nearing my face holding a mascara brush. Black inked my eyelashes. I forced myself to remain still.

After what felt like an eternity, I stood in the most exquisite and decorative outfit of my life. Standing with other young women in exquisite and decorative dresses, dysphoria washed over me like a particularly rainy day.

But the sun was shining brightly through the hollow window, and the Choosing Ceremony was for Unfortunates.

"Do you love it, or do you *LOVE* it?" Fern squealed.

I couldn't trust my words, my focus split between the butterfly pendant resting on my neck and the Fairaway servant who dressed me this way. Most of the servants left the room except for Mercy and Amelia, who were standing silently in the background, waiting for their next task.

Sunflowers arched in Persephone's black hair, representing beauty and impermanence. Each yellow petal highlighted the keen twinkle in the Mati's eyes, and her dark red lips resembled a budding rose. The yellow dress sat tightly against her chest before cascading down her tall body. The sleeves hung loosely on her muscular arms, starting at the top hem and moving down to her wrists to reveal her large shoulders and collar bone.

Fern, standing even taller in green-leaved heels, wore a short brown romper that showed off her large thighs and long legs. Her red strands secured in two braids that clung to her head and laid against her chest. Hands on her hips, Fern imitated the oak tree for strength.

Delilah's strawberry blonde hair tied in a fishtail braid that laid softly on her left side. Fern created several dark blue flowers to intertwine within her hair. Her petite blue dress was lined with wire to extend outward from her body, and her eyelids reflected the violent thunderstorms on hot summer nights. She represented water for patience and concentration, though I didn't know if that matched her personality all too well.

Skylar nailed the most bizarre outfit. Her blonde hair wrapped in a loose bun with two flyaway pieces curled above her arched eyebrows. Though she wore a simple brown dress that revealed the thin zigzag scars along her forearm, that wasn't what brought any attention. Feathered wings of brown and gold and red expanded out from her back and framed her body, matching the brown undertones of her face and golden lips. Eyeliner illuminated her shark eyes, and she twirled around in admiration of herself, representing the owl and certainly not the mouse in the life cycle duo.

Black draped Molly's pale skin, covering her entire form and representing the moon for darkness as she sat in the corner and looked at the sky. I imagined how her younger sister Melanie would look in a bright yellow dress that represented the sun for light—just like the one I dressed her in when Mr. Harris arrived to the Montgomery manor.

I was the only Unfortunate in an outfit. Deep purple wings engulfed my body, lined black and dotted with white to represent the butterfly for change. My satin short dress was the same deep purple color split into two pieces: a heart-shaped top and skirt, and I instinctually covered my exposed skin with my arms. Black flats snuggly wrapped around my feet.

"I certainly love it." Skylar twirled and looked to the door with her hands on her hips, "Now where can I find Leo? Persephone, come with me. We need to show off."

Fern grabbed my hand and turned me away from the mirror.

In the living room, Leo complimented his sister while trying to personally sabotage the intensive Unfortunate work given to Skylar's hair. The Aura's hand received a mild burn when snatching his wrist, and Fern desperately tried to hide herself from the flash of her mother's camera.

"That's *it*!"

Turning to Skylar's voice, I watched Leo disappear out of the open window and descend the equivalent of ten stories. The Aura straightened from her violent stance, putting her nose in the air and taking a deep breath.

"Is my hair okay?" she asked.

Persephone nodded, her arms crossed and unmoving.

"Skylar!" I ran over to the window.

"What?!" Skylar crossed her arms defensively. "He totally deserved that!"

"Pers—" I couldn't read her blank expression, "why aren't you—he's going to die!"

"Oh, please," Skylar rolled her eyes, spinning her finger as I looked down. "He hasn't hit the ground."

Indeed, he hadn't.

Leo hovered mid-air near the ground, his body bouncing lightly to the small whirlpool-like air pocket Skylar made with the twirl of her index finger. Even at a far distance, the small curl of his lips betrayed his narrowed stare as if he deserved his punishment. He stuck his tongue out at us.

Skylar scoffed at the unruly gesture, releasing her hand and walking away, no longer amused. Leo landed on his back and waved to us still looking down.

Persephone and I waved back. "How did you know she wouldn't kill him?" I asked.

"Skylar warned me beforehand," she replied matter-of-factly. "And I don't blame her. He likes egging her on."

"Warned?" My thoughts spilled out loud. That didn't sound like Skylar at all. "They've been acting stranger since their run in with Ebony Nique at the Determination Arena. I understand Skylar's hostility because Leo saved her, but...do you know anything?"

Persephone shrugged, "Don't know. Neither of them will tell me any details."

CHAPTER FIVE

The Flower Festival

We headed to the Flower Festival at the bazaar separate from Princess Maya who wanted to watch the festivities from atop it all in a private box designed for her. She refused my direct presence and took Mercy instead alongside several Royal Crest Knights. I offered to remain on the ground-level as a futile effort to continue my personal guard duties, but she refused that too.

Trees covered in bright flower arrangements towered over the festival clearing. Constantly on the brink of an earthquake, the ground swayed beneath my feet as Avlis in all sorts of crazy and interesting outfits cheered, danced, and walked around.

Shopkeepers sold colorful masks, costumes, and flowered decorations to winding lines. Mouths moved and jumbled with other voices. Even if Cassius could find me here, I didn't think I could hear him.

Everyone dispersed to go on their own adventures together; Fern led my hand through the chaos.

"Come on!" Fern pulled my arm. "We can make it to the plant sculpture competition!"

My feet dragged along the dirt. *We weren't even supposed to be here right now,* I thought.

Pastel pinks, yellows as bright as the sun, and all shades of green overwhelmed my sight as we passed by flower sellers, flower buyers, and flower exchangers. Heat clung to my skin along with the new summer air, and Gifteds in similar costumes complimented us on our attire.

We made it to a small clearing roped off for the event. Avlis participants stood inside square boxes painted in the grass by Unfortunate servants. Fern released me and ran over to sign up for the competition.

The competition host handed her seeds, and she jumped into her designated space. I remained nearby within the surrounding crowd.

The horn blared, and the plant sculpture competition began. Avlis lifted the dirt beneath them and rotated their wrists as they cultivated their pieces.

Fern hit the ground and intentionally dispersed seeds parallel to each other on the left and right side. Squatting, she cupped her hands together and gently released her right hand from her left. Stems sprouted from the dirt and intertwined as one budded red and the other white and repeated. Fern steadily rose as her right arm continued rising above her head. Her left hand followed the path of her right until both palms met once more on the opposite side. She stopped, the flower arch complete.

Fern sighed, stepping back and admiring her work behind the sun's glare. Her arms fell to her side and glistened with sweat as she caught her breath. Emerald eyes found me.

"What do you think?"

I smiled and gestured her closer with my finger. "I think you should look your best when you win first prize."

"Oh, is there something on my face?" Fern covered her cheeks with her hands but failed to wipe anything away. "Did I get it?"

I struggled against her insistence to do it herself. "Let me," I asked in a light voice.

Her eyes squinted as she processed my request, but she leaned down anyway.

"My dress doesn't have enough fabric so—" I wiped away dirt from her nose with my thumb. "There. Now I can see your freckles again."

Fern's cheeks crinkled as she smiled. "Have you always been this cute?"

I bit the inside of my cheek but failed to keep my face neutral. "Why did you choose those flowers?" I changed the subject.

Red and white flooded my vision. Two flowers. Combined by their interwoven stems.

"Unity flowers are my favorite," she chirped. "Happens when red poppies and white peonies grow together. Did you have a better idea?"

I shook my head, continuing to stare as their contrast as the judges made their rounds.

Fern won a bronze metal, and we celebrated with festival food. Flowers pressed into any sweet we could find: orchids in shortbread, rose petals and hibiscus in cocktails, and marigold at the center of lollipops. But Fern's favorite was honey and lavender ice cream. Our scoops melted quickly, and I laughed watching Fern struggle to eat every last drop before it fell off the cone.

The day stretched on.

Fern led me through her culture's vibrancy, and I watched her succeed in everything she put her mind to. The power race was a no holds barred event where Gifteds sprinted down a track, using their Gifts to their fullest advantage to reach the end first. She challenged other Avlis by tossing a long tapered pole using the earth below, and she rivaled Skylar in a rock climbing competition.

The sun brought the sky to an orange hue in its descent. Fern looked to me, saying, "Is there anything you would like to do?"

I glanced around. "What could I do that isn't Gift related?"

Fern pouted before her eyes lightened. "I have an idea."

We arrived at a booth not as densely packed as the others. Thin fiber and dried grass in an assortment of colors lined the table, and several older Gifted women wove the ribbons into baskets. A person in the middle waited patiently for anyone who might need assistance. I was surprised that none of them had a branded U on their hand. This looked like Unfortunate work.

We approached and sat down. Fern sat on my right side so none of the Gifteds around us could see my brand from a passing glance. Instructions laid out on a piece of paper in front of us. My lessons with Princess Maya were still so new...

"Fern, could you tell me what this says?" I asked.

She leaned forward and did, and she only needed to do that once for me to understand. Fern, on the other hand, glanced from her hands to the instructions and back again for several minutes before attempting her first move.

The person in the middle looked at the Avlis. "Do you need help getting started?"

"No, no," Fern waved her off. "I got it."

I repeated the pattern in its exact order; Fern missed a

couple of steps. Her eyes drifted to my hands with an intensity Kai would hope she'd use for her studies. Her face hardened as she grew impatient with herself, and her face softened as she tried to silently calm herself down. I couldn't help but stare. She was so bubbly and effortlessly confident in everything else we did today.

Finally, she spoke. "How are you doing that so well?"

I shrugged. "I'm just treating this as a task. Kind of like when I was at the Montgomery House. There was a lot I had to learn myself. And anytime I failed, I was punished."

"So you're used to doing things all yourself, too?"

I stopped fiddling with my basket. "Absolutely not."

Fern noticed the sternness in my voice and looked at me.

I continued, "When Valerie was brought home, my life as a servant became tolerable. I could depend on another to help me with the chores, attend to Mrs. Montgomery's every whim, protect me from the rain..."

"The rain?"

"Yeah, I'm sure your servants have their own trauma from the Choosing Ceremony."

I replied so sharply, time halted for several heartbeats. How was she going to respond to that slicing comment?

"I wouldn't know," Fern admitted in a soft voice. "I've never been to a Choosing Ceremony. We've only taken in servants from Houses that were outwardly antagonistic or abusive. Amelia, for example, was given to numerous Houses before my mom took her in. And I hope Poppy is okay. I don't know what she's been through, but when she first arrived, my mom asked the other girls to tend to her bruises before she could start working."

What? I thought. I had never heard of such an act of mercy from Gifteds. When Valerie was maimed by Molly for my mistake, the Montgomerys still expected the same quickness to their demands as though she was healthy.

When I remained quiet, Fern continued. She looked down at her misshapen basket as though lost in thought.

"I want to be as strong as my mother. She raised me and Delilah all by herself, and she's saved more Unfortunates than any Gifted finds respectable. If I can make her proud..."

She bit down on her lip as it quivered.

"Well," I reached for her misshapen basket and started tucking in the loose strands, "no one truly does anything alone."

Valerie and I needed each other at the Montgomery House. I needed Mr. Harris to attend Galdor Academy. Mr. Harris needed Prince Cassius to teach me how to fight. Prince Cassius needed Mr. Harris's Gift to become king. And the AGM needed a king with the Divine's power who could give us the equality we so desperately deserved.

We stared off in silence.

"Hey, would you like to make chocolate chip cookies when we get back?" Fern prompted. "Amelia never lets me cook for myself. Says it's too much sugar. Like I have too much sugar. Do you think I have too much sugar? I can handle it. Can you handle it?"

A chuckle rose in my throat, "I would love to."

CHAPTER SIX

Property of the Fairaway House

Princess Maya refused my presence again, taking Mercy and several Royal Crest Knights with her to watch the festivities from her private box. She was a safe distance away sitting atop the trees, peering out to take in all the events, the citizens, and the flowers from a safe distance. She was a safe distance away.

As everyone else left for the next day's festivities, Fern and I baked chocolate chip cookies. It reminded me of the times you and I made cookies for Melanie and stole two for ourselves.

We were never as messy as Fern, though. She violently sloshed the wet and dry ingredients for the prep time to go faster, and chips carelessly scattered the floor when she playfully threw them at me after I told her she put too many in the mix.

After she ravaged the cookies, I insisted Fern leave the

dishes to me before she somehow flooded the house with soap water. She went on ahead to the festival, eager to bring back some shortbread cookies so we could replicate them later.

Kai came back to the house. He noticed me in the kitchen and rolled up his sleeves. "May I help?"

My eyebrows arched in slight confusion, "Sure."

The Mare stepped toward the sink, and I side-stepped so he could stand next to me. He stared expectantly at the plate in my hand. "You clean, I dry?"

Realizing my awkward stare with wide eyes, I plunged the plate back into the water and scrubbed it clean.

Slowly handing him the dish, I watched him wave his free hand. The water ripped away from the plate in one quick stream and fell into the drain. He set the clean plate on top of the others before turning back and starring expectantly.

My eyes flickered several times before we began the process over again.

"Would you prefer solitude?" asked Kai.

I shook my head, giving him a fork.

"Hand me the rest of the utensils," he instructed.

I scrubbed a whisk. "I just—I've never worked with a Gifted like this."

Kai scoffed, fiddling with his new collection. The water separated with the flick of his wrist. "I've never worked with an Unfortunate like this. I'm often home alone while my mom works, so I'm used to doing the house chores."

"Is that why you're nice to me?"

Kai scoffed again in a shaky voice, his shoulders scrunching closer to his body.

"Were you always this forward?"

A small smile flashed my face. I reached for the mixing bowl. "No, I wasn't."

We cleaned in silence. I rummaged the water for any new plates. "In any case, I won't press if you don't—"

"You're," Kai's shoulders raised in a sharp inhale and then lowered in a rough exhale, "fine."

I looked at him, but he kept his eyes on his work. "It's not something I like talking about. Let's just say that Skylar was right when she said I was lucky enough to have a last name. 'Lancer' doesn't mean much now, but..."

He trailed off, setting another dish down. "It will one day."

The stillness in his face refused to display the entanglement of thought behind his eyes. If Kai managed to detangle those thoughts, would he unravel?

He certainly wasn't alone, hoping that his name would mean something more. We all were in our own ways. I didn't tell him, though. Working together, side by side like this, already spoke volumes.

"You started double studying as an ERS intern," I noted. "How is that going?"

"My feet are definitely sore," Kai admitted light-heartedly.

"Would you like a chair?"

"No need—we're almost done."

We finished the dishes. My back prickled as Amelia tip-toed into the kitchen. She outstretched her hands to Kai. "Allow me to put those away, sir."

"I got it." He stretched his body to reach the top shelf.

"I insist, sir." She turned to me with a neutral expression. "You too, ma'am."

I halted as Kai pushed the plates back and lowered to the ground. He brushed off his fingers and glanced from me to the other Unfortunate.

"Sure thing. Thank you."

She tilted her head as we passed.

My back prickled again. Unfortunates clung to the walls, hiding in the darkness like I used to do. I stopped walking.

"I think I'm going to stay here for a little longer. I'll see you at the festival, Kai."

His eyes squinted at the sudden shift in my voice but he didn't press. "See you, Nora."

We listened to his footsteps retreat and the front door close. I turned behind me and the Fairaway servant who dressed me in Gifted clothes revealed herself.

My mouth twitched, ready to ask what was going on, when she exchanged a look that said *'follow me'* instead.

An Unfortunate servant's best weapon was what we could say in silence. My slight eye twitch said I would cautiously oblige.

We walked down a stretch of corridor on the second floor of the house and arrived at a room away from the others. She lightly tapped on the doorframe. The door opened a crack before swinging open.

A tight grasp pulled me in, and the door strategically closed behind us, the knob turning slowly to avoid any detection that it moved at all.

Light poured through the glassless open window, illuminating six of the Fairaway servants. Their head servant was still in the kitchen.

Nerves haunted their frigid movements and twiddling fingers. As I gazed at their faces, they kept their heads half-lowered.

One Unfortunate in particular was constantly circling the room, throwing sand into the open air and letting it fall to the ground.

"What are you doing?" I asked.

"Sanding," the Unfortunate closest to me responded, "in

case the young Miss Delilah sneaks in here invisibly."

"Oh," I occupied a few heartbeats to ruffle out my clothes as the silence crept back in.

"She's not here right now," whispered the Unfortunate with the bag of sand as she continued to circle the room anyway.

Everyone turned to me: Iridion's first Unfortunate soldier.

"How did you escape?" one of the shorter ones asked.

Escape? I almost scoffed. I didn't feel like I escaped anything. My life still belonged to Gifteds, and plenty were ready to kill me.

"*Promise me, Nora.*"

Wait.

"*You'll escape at any chance you get.*"

How could I be so hasty in my thoughts?

"A Royal Crest Knight, Mr. Harris, offered me this life. I made a promise to leave servitude if given the opportunity."

"The man who recruited Miss Fern?" one asked.

Their questions ricocheted off the other. "Why would he do that? Is that why he talked to Poppy? Is that why she left? Tell us, why *you*?"

Some stepped forward with raised eyebrows, hanging onto my every word. I hadn't thought about how Mr. Harris searched for an Unfortunate to help his cause before he found me. Knowing how he could read minds when we first met, I wondered what he saw in Poppy's character. Where was she now?

"I don't know," I confessed. "It might have to do with how I reacted to a run-in with a small faction of the Anti-Gifteds Movement."

The Unfortunates gasped, stepping back and pressing closer to each other.

Alarm widened my eyes. "Have you encountered them?"

There was a nodded consensus. "Sometimes, when we're out doing tasks for Ms. Fairaway, we're approached by other servants who fled their Houses."

"They're here?"

"Always recruiting," one piped up in a soft voice. "That's why Poppy left. She joined them."

"Amelia keeps telling us that it's such a disgrace."

"Amelia doesn't know what she's talking about."

"But Ms. Fairaway has always been kind to us. We're really lucky to have her."

"I wouldn't blame you for joining." I jolted, surprised how easy those words rang with my voice. "I know that the Anti-Gifteds Movement looks promising; that it will give us what we've always deserved. But…"

My words drifted off for a moment, thinking about Sylvia Douglas hanging from a pole. "You know, I met an Unfortunate named Sylvia Douglas. Maybe you saw her in the news?"

"Do you mean Douglas was her House name?"

"No," I shook my head. "I think she had a last name."

One Unfortunate scoffed, "We don't have last names."

"But she did!" I insisted. "Either she gave it to herself or the Anti-Gifteds Movement gave it to her."

The servants squinted with bewilderment. "Why are you telling us this?"

I opened my mouth for a quick answer, but justification couldn't find itself in my mind.

"It's fantastic and exciting to have a title, but there is something wrong with the movement. It's led by a Gifted, by the Diviner."

The last word slipped out like bile, and the Unfortunates

shifted on edge.

"Then what are we supposed to do?" they asked.

Their eyes stared into mine, waiting for me to give them hope. My hesitation clung to the walls like plastic wrap. What *was* I supposed to tell these girls? What could I possibly tell them that would keep them safe outside a Gifted House so unusually kind?

We were always doomed from the start.

I knew the sword resting beside me was a fluke; an impossibly lucky chance in my meeting Mr. Harris. An impossibly lucky chance in my offering to Galdor Academy. An impossibly lucky chance in my survival there.

What could I possibly tell *myself* that blossomed hope?

The sudden sound of fire, disturbed earth, and intense air could have fooled me into thinking I held one of three Gifts, for those destructive interruptions were all too familiar now.

All of the Fairaway servants screamed and held on to each other. I wrapped my fingers around my sword defensively. "Stay here."

"*Is it the Diviner?*"

I bumped lightly into the door before opening it, swallowing hard at the thought.

"Stay here," I repeated with more urgency.

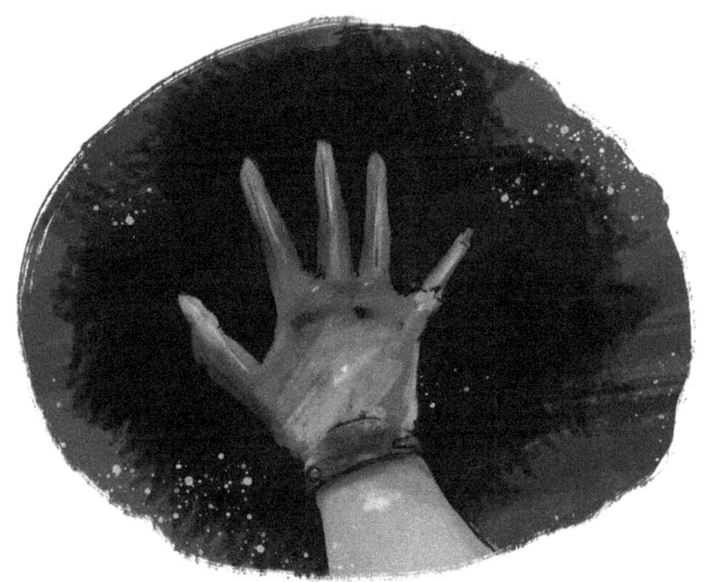

CHAPTER SEVEN

Red Poppy

Black smoke rose through the canopy.

As I descended down the wooden stairs designated to servants, time passed faster with my accelerated heartbeat. I couldn't use the wind or the grass or even the condensation to my advantage. My feet alone propelled me forward.

People already scattered along the forest floor, running away from the blast. It had to be the AGM. Of course, they couldn't miss this opportunity. So many Gifteds in one place...

Could I be...could I be running right to him?

My pace slowed.

If I was...I begged I wouldn't have to alone.

I quickened. Faces blurred past me. None I recognized as my friends. Closer to the festival clearing, panic deafened my ears. My body twisted and contorted as I maneuvered the dense crowd. I searched for a flash of red—of fire or cloth or hair.

I continued pushing through, one foot in front of the other. *There!*

I reached out to catch her, but she caught back as if searching for me too. We spun and halted, using our grip on the other to stabilize ourselves.

I noticed the distinct U scar burned into her hand and a red-laced ribbon around her throat. We strained to pull the other inward.

"What have you done?" I demanded. "Where is the princess?"

"I'm given strict orders to keep you away from reaching her," replied the AGM Unfortunate.

Orders? Did that mean... "Is he really here?"

The Unfortunate raised her other arm up, revealing a large mallet. She swung where our hands connected; I gasped and unlatched. The mallet swayed through the air; we stumbled back.

I didn't have time to fight her. If what she said was true, I needed to reach the princess *now*!

Turning around, I collided with several people at once. Gifteds used me as a way to drive themselves forward, pressing their hands along my shoulder, back, and sides. Why weren't they using their Gift?

Another hand gripped my shoulder. The AGM Unfortunate spun me around and pushed me on my back.

Pressing her weight onto my hips, her mallet dug near inches from my head. Struggling was to no avail.

Clenching my fist, I realized that my sword was no longer in my possession.

The AGM rebel squealed as though excited, "It's nice to finally meet you, Nora! I'm Poppy. I haven't chosen a last name, either—"

I thrashed, but she continued, "What do you think goes with Poppy? My mother thought that giving me an Avlis first name would win me favor, but I don't really want an Avlis House name."

She reached for something a little ways off, her legs long enough to keep me in place. So this was the servant that ran away from the Fairaways. From what Fern told me yesterday, there was more darkness behind that childlike smile. What did Mr. Harris see in her?

My sword glistened as it came into view. As Poppy observed the craftsmanship, she read off the Iridion Code, "I solemnly swear to uphold the integrity of the Third Auran Reign and all Reigns before and thereafter."

It didn't matter why—I didn't have time for this. I needed to reach Maya! I knew exactly where the private box was. I was too close now to let this Unfortunate beat me.

Blood trickled down Poppy's arm. I gasped at the sight as she created a clean and careful incision in her left arm. The AGM Unfortunate took two fingers, pressing into her wound, and more blood oozed out. A droplet splattering against my face like rain.

Poppy delicately moved her bloodied fingers against the sword and admired her work.

We locked eyes again. "Do you like it?"

The blood of the violent rebellion dripped downwards, but the message was clear: *UNFORTUNATE*

When I responded in resistance, she pressed the sword against my throat. I instinctually tried to move my chin away, but it only served to expose my neck more.

"Why do you fight for them?" she asked. "Why follow an incompetent princess who isn't even near the throne?"

I grabbed a pressure point.

"Ow!"

The imbalance was enough for my right arm to break free and grab ahold of the large mallet. Tossing the object with all my might, I kicked Poppy away.

Standing, I glanced for any weaponry on the ground nearby.

Poppy still held my sword in a tight grasp, pointing it straight at my heart. "How do they train you at Galdor Academy?"

We glanced to the large mallet off center. I charged, sliding across the ground to reach the weapon first. Poppy plunged the sword downwards.

The mallet was heavier than I anticipated, but I countered the sword's path above my head before the fumble cost my life.

The AGM soldier then attacked my torso; I blocked the first blow with the mallet's steel rod. She sliced the air over and over again, pushing me back with each swing.

The sword came forward straight on. Metal grazed my cheek as I tried to dodge. Blood trickled down my face as Poppy closed the distance. Crouching, I used the rod to push the other Unfortunate over my body.

Poppy gasped and fell awkwardly, dropping the sword in the process. But she was quick and picked it back up before I could make my next move.

Her breath hot and rapid, the AGM soldier lunged forward again; I adjusted the mallet accordingly. The blade wedged itself into the rubber, and Poppy inhaled sharply at what she had done.

I jerked away from the other Unfortunate, effectively taking both weapons for myself. I ripped the sword out of the mallet, dropped her useless weapon to the ground, and held a defensive stance.

"Where is Maya?" I demanded again. "What have you done to her?"

Poppy looked up to the trees that surrounded the clearing. I did too—I saw how the branches wilted, how the leaves darkened, blackened, and became ash until the entire tree turned into nothing.

No. I was all too familiar with what that meant.

"She wanted to reach her people."

My eyes met Poppy's, and her grin widened. "We just reminded her that she never can."

I ran away, closer and closer to the center of the festival, to the private box that held Princess Maya—the one that peered out to watch all of the events, the citizens, and flowers from a safe distance. She was a safe distance!

Fewer and fewer civilians were left running away from their princess. I halted as I caught sight of her, frozen in a fallen position and staring at her gloved hand pressed to the ground.

Reaching her would be impossible. A poisoned earth surrounded her open palm, casting every blade of grass into an inky black void that consumed the festival in its wake. Abandoned tents and their flowers and prizes and carefully crafted decorations now collapsed and molded into black masses, unrecognizable of their original celebration. Event placement lines and first place winner showcases crumbled to dust. Tree trunks thinned and rotted away.

The private box was nowhere to be found—any evidence of its existence removed from this world. The only thing that remained was Princess Maya, unmoving, at the epicenter.

The poison crept forward, sinking the next closest organic matter.

I watched, unable to step forward and unwilling to turn back.

It took two hours for the poison to stop, and another half-hour before Princess Maya finally stood upright. Our eyes met.

She approached me. Her head lowered; her face grey and sunken. She stopped at the line between blackened ash and green grass, between her Gift and my lack thereof.

In a soft, haunted voice, she begged, "Remove me from this place."

White and red petals stretched out for infinity in front of my eyes, swaying alongside the wind. Cassius sat at the center with his back facing me.

"Will you dance with me, Nora?"

"No."

"Would you sit with me, perhaps?" His light tone didn't change, twisting a unity flower between his careful, methodical fingers.

I raced forward, halting at the edge of the flower line. "How did you find us?"

Cassius's posture didn't change. "I can find you anywhere, especially through those who serve me."

He turned so we could see each other, a peaceful expression unfitting on his face. "With enough time and patience, I can do anything."

My chest burned as anger filled my voice. "Why did—?"

"Your turn."

A sword appeared in my hand and another appeared dormant across his crossed knees. *UNFORTUNATE* obscured my sight in the sword's reflection, written in Poppy's blood—the same mark I vigorously cleaned off as we returned to Galdor. I huffed at the reminder. This time, I would kill him.

His shoulders slouched in a deep sigh as I charged him.

But as I swung, Cassius swung back with a blow that threw me backwards. I fell on my palms.

He stood slowly, waiting.

Throwing myself upwards, I slashed diagonally. Cassius stared intensely at my movements, his sword gliding off mine as he blocked.

"Your attacks could be more fluid," he commented.

An irritable growl reverberated in my throat as a response, striking several jabs and pushing him back.

I closed the distance, our weapons crossed close to the helm. "Who is Poppy to you?" I demanded.

He raised an eyebrow, leaning closer between the two blades. "Are you jealous?"

I gasped, "No!" Stepping back, I angled my sword straight at his smirk.

"Oh, Nora."

He pushed my sword away from my body and turned his weapon horizontally. The point pressed along the dip between my collarbones. Its cool touch ran chills down my spine and held me in place like his Animus Gift.

Shaking, my sword slipped easily from my hands as Cassius swung and drove it downwards. He pulled me into him, my back pressed against his stomach and his blade pressed against my throat within a blink of an eye—if I could blink, if I could move, if I could do anything but stay paralyzed in fear. My skin stitched apart as he traced a line across my neck. Blood as bright as an AGM band trickled down my chest and dampened my clothes.

My breaths hitched; my arms stiffened and my legs threatened to collapse. Cassius released his sword to the unity flowers and wrapped himself securely around my frame.

"You're my brightest Unfortunate."

CHAPTER EIGHT

A Princess's Coronation

He called me "the brightest Unfortunate" before.

I remembered when his face was so close to mine I couldn't look away. I remembered how dark his eyes were and how intense his stare was and the exact way his face folded into wrinkles when he playfully squinted and asked if I was really an Unfortunate.

You're just so incredibly bright is all, he explained. *You're so different from what I'm used to.*

Stop.

Stop thinking about what he was.

The Determination rolled its way into my thoughts like a thunderstorm. It was raining that night too when Cassius revealed himself as the Diviner. I remembered how his face flashed into a white hue from a lightning strike overhead and the exact way his face hardened when I reminded him of his sister and told him I was afraid.

It's unfitting for someone so much brighter than her, he

recoiled. *You understand more than anyone else why the world doesn't need leaders like her.*

I remembered every detail so perfectly. Cassius had to be using his Gift to aid in my torment, weaving through my memories with delicate, purposeful hands. Why else would everything stick to my mind the same way your death did?

What does he see in me—his brightest Unfortunate?

Looking up to Princess Maya—the one who ran away from her problems in Northbrook, the one who allowed another Unfortunate Law to take root, the one who remained neutral while Unfortunates continued to suffer, and all ready in costume alone for her coronation day—I desperately wanted her to be more. To prove Cassius wrong and stop the entire kingdom from unraveling with me.

"I can't do this."

My stomach tightened. Coronation preparations and Norburn patrols were happening around the clock for the past two weeks. No three. The past three weeks.

I tried to sound encouraging. "You're already dressed."

"I can't do this."

Patrols either reported nothing or came back injured and weakened from a violent city who despised them. Inhabitants of the crime capitol were growing ever-restless from royal intervention. They terrorized troops and hurled insults at their princess in place of the Diviner. Any back door cooperation or loosely promised alliances for information didn't exist.

I pressed past the doubt. "You're going to be fine."

"I can't do this."

And the Flower Festival. It was like she was still stuck in that fallen position, staring at the desolate earth she poisoned.

"You have nothing to fear. The papers promised not to publish anything about the accident."

"Don't call it an accident," she shifted her default response, flexing her fingers beneath brand-new gloves. "When the bomb denoted, I thought Cassius sent them to kill me but..."

She stared at her pinkie—where the blast shredded the fabric away, "He knew what I really feared most."

Princess Maya's frown deepened. "That festival meant so much to those people. And I... I destroyed it."

"They can rebuild," I said quickly. "And that means we can, too. With you as our rightful leader."

"You're forgetting Prince Henry."

"With you as our *regent*, then."

The princess returned to her reflection. "I can't do this."

My lungs deflated.

She continued, "Minister Gabriel should become regent in my place."

"Out of the question." I wouldn't entertain the thought.

A pitiful smile formed on Princess Maya's lips as she lowered her head. "I imagine you would rather Cassius than the minister."

She waited in that silence, refusing to look at me. Princess Maya twisted her body away from the mirror, her lips tightly wound in frustration. She stood, fiddling her fingers.

"I would rather you as regent, ma'am," I finally said.

She paced in a small circle before catching sight of the window and freezing in place. Like an Unfortunate triggered by her Choosing Ceremony, the princess stared through the glass for more heartbeats than I cared to count. The sun shined, so I didn't join her.

"Please, Maya," I searched for the right words, "talk to me."

She straightened her posture and folded her hands in front of herself before turning her entire body toward me. Standing in her coronation dress, Princess Maya radiated the same comfortability she held in her fighting attire at the Determination Arena—that is, none at all.

A heart-shaped neckline exposed her collarbones and the short sleeves rested off her shoulders, exposing her slender arms too. Despite her desperate attempts otherwise, Minister Gabriel insisted that tradition be upheld and she wear the dress all queens wore to a coronation, recreated perfectly to accommodate Princess Maya's Gift in material alone.

Cinched at the waist, the body of the dress flowed outward and stretched out on the floor in lace. Gold lined the cream-colored dress in complex floral patterns along the waist and hem. Gloves of the same color and design covered her up to her wrists. The same deep purple color held over the hearts of Senior Royal Crest Knights colored her jewels.

"I've been preparing for this moment for my entire existence. I know all of Iridion history, every Gifted House deemed necessary to learn, every curtsy or law ordinance. Every..."

She tried to find another example and gestured to her dress instead, "I feel like I'm in a costume. In some sort of tragic play."

I raised an eyebrow. "Where is the princess who spoke with all the qualities of a queen at her parents' funeral?"

"Those are qualities I wish to hold. The reason why I decided to go to Northbrook was so I could obtain all the qualities of a queen. Before I am crowned, I want to reach my people."

She looked out the window again. "I thought I would have more time to achieve that goal. I want to feel close to those I'm supposed to serve. Be among them despite the risk. But..."

But everyone fled from her, fearful of her Gift. Fearful of a power she actively hated. And the AGM made sure she remembered.

"How can I be an effective leader if I can't reach my subjects? How can I justify my position when I'm unattainable? Even by those closest to me, I can't physically reach them."

She sighed in deep frustration.

Valerie and I always went out of our way to touch each other: brushing sides meant *I'm here* and elbow bumps meant *look* or *stop* or *halt*; if our fingers or arms interlocked that meant *let's do this together* and a quick kick to the ankle meant *careful*. We survived that way, protected each other that way.

I thought about my Gifted classmates and how Fern liked to hug me to no end, how easily Persephone could pick me up and run away, how Kai examined our ailments, how Leo and Skylar often collided in conflict, and even how Molly, now more withdrawn than ever, was becoming more and more unattainable to my understanding.

I realized how far Princess Maya was to me—a safe distance.

I stared at her gloves sealing her Gift from the outside world.

Apprehension seeped through my nerves. Could I really bring myself to touch her hand after all I've witnessed?

She rushed back to the mirror before I could decide. Her gloves pressed against the dresser, and her shoulders slouched as they often did these past three weeks. Princess Maya bent lower, her head staring downward and eyes tightly shut. As she prayed, I remained silent.

She opened her eyes. "Okay," she inhaled slowly, "I will do it."

I snapped my attention to her, our eyes locking from the mirror's reflection.

"Really?" I breathed and then quickly recovered, "I'm so glad to hear that, ma'am."

"Yes well," Princess Maya didn't sound excited for her choice, "I will do anything to no longer be burdened by this Gift."

***

Cameras circled Princess Maya and the throne room. A small group of elite government members were presented on film. The world needed to know that their queen was established and would hold Divine jurisdiction. We needed to use Cassius's trick against him.

I stayed on guard in the formal military outfit, watching the ceremony from the doorway. I couldn't make out what Minister Gabriel was saying, but I was more concerned by another.

The world is watching. Will you attack? I asked for the 100th time.

No. Cassius promised. *She shall become queen.*

I didn't believe him. Why would he allow her to become queen when he was so adamant that she shouldn't?

Five men in distinctly colored robes stood on either side of Minister Gabriel; the regional ministers Princess Maya mentioned before. They were one of the reasons she allowed Minister Gabriel's 8th ULS to pass. All looked as pretentious as their leader; noses raised and misguided as righteous.

As I watched Princess Maya slowly walk up to Minister Gabriel, she did her best to hide her fears in front of the flashing lights and cameras. But the small flex of her gloves told me she was exerting all her nerves through her hidden fingers.

Her breathing appeared regulated as the minister spoke from the Great Book and poured oil along the princess' forehead.

You can reach me, I thought. *You can reach your people.*

Cassius scoffed in my mind, and the throne room vanished before my eyes. My surroundings transformed into a familiar house; I glanced around frantically in hopes of figuring out where. Could this be a memory bleeding into my waking thoughts?

Ascending upstairs through my sight but remaining completely still in reality, I dismissed this as the Montgomery house. But it was a manor, I realized. One I hadn't set foot in for over a year now. The Crawfords resided here, the House closest to the Montgomerys an hour away from their summer home. Why was Cassius showing me this?

I recognized the bronze railing distinct from the Montgomery's silver one, but I never stepped foot upstairs. I was always confined downstairs, helping the Crawford servants make lunch. How was Cassius showing me this if those memories didn't exist?

Opening a door on the second level revealed Poppy sitting with her body turned away and in front of several stuffed animals. That didn't make sense. If Cassius was showing me my memories, Poppy couldn't be here. She belonged to the Fairaways in Northbrook. I would remember her from my time working in Cherryville. This couldn't be a memory at all. It's—

"Where's Mora?"

As Poppy turned to face the opened door, Melanie Montgomery caught my vision. She looked in my direction, her lips pouted and arms crossed around a snake stuffed animal.

Dread sank into my heart and rose in my chest like bile. A sickness brought my forehead to a burn.

"Don't worry, Miss Melanie." Cassius's soft voice came from my point of view.

Approaching her, a hand reached out like it was attached to my body. It wasn't mine. I recognized his from all the times he offered a dance. I was seeing through Cassius's perspective, seeing him pick up Melanie in his arms.

She hardly grew at all during the last year, appearing almost the same as she did when I left her for Galdor. Her Lux eyes were as wide as ever, staring into Cassius and therefore staring into me.

"She's coming soon."

The throne room came back into focus, and Queen Maya stood in front of the centered throne, adorned with the sovereign's crown. Avlis created petals that fell from either side of the throne, careful not to sprinkle directly under her lest they burn and disintegrate from her touch. Her advisors and guards cheered to her health and leadership; a gentle smile lightened Queen Maya's face.

I couldn't indulge in the celebration.

If you hurt her Cassius—

I will do no such thing, he soothed. *As long as you do exactly as I say.*

I needed to warn Molly. Make up some excuse for her to reach back out and check on Melanie. My feet turned to leave.

Stop.

Jolting, my fingers pressed onto the wall's corner and held me there.

You will not give her or any of the others hints, instructed Cassius. *And you will stay within Galdor Academy's walls until night falls tomorrow.*

Tomorrow? Every fiber in my being propelled me toward the exit. I needed to reach Melanie now. Reach her before...before...I couldn't even bring myself to say it.

You will wait or I will take her Gift.

No. No no no no no. The only reason we even knew he could take Gifts was because Molly held enough strength to survive the process. She felt her soul rip out and became empty. So many others died before her. I couldn't risk Melanie's life so needlessly.

He knew my answer before I could accept.

See you soon.

CHAPTER NINE

The Divine Observer

———

Queen Maya threw the newspaper down onto the Senior Circle desk and stared at those bold black letters as the headline read:

DIVINITY POISONED BY NEW QUEEN

"They're all over the city, ma'am," Isaac Winters explained, "showcasing what happened at the Flower Festival."

"Yes, I can see that." Queen Maya's tone was short, tapping her index finger against her leg. She stared at herself—greyed and surrounded by an inky black sea that darkened the page.

"And subsequently, they're calling for the Diviner as rightful head of state. Among other reasons."

"Yes, thank you, Mr. Winters."

Isaac stared with a tightened expression, understanding that he should stop talking. He nodded, "Your Majesty."

Tossing and turning the night before, I finally understood

why Cassius wanted me to wait until today to rescue Melanie. All so he could launch this new attack: an AGM newspaper. All so he could hear his sister's reaction through my mind. Witness her unravel through my waning heart.

"Your Majesty, there's nothing to worry about," Minister Gabriel promised. "Gifteds will see this as the blasphemy it is. The AGM committed the crime. The damage wasn't purposeful by your hand. No legitimate claims shall be held in high regard against you."

"Yes, minister, but it was still my hand," Queen Maya's voice shook, flexing her glove in jagged movements. "It doesn't matter whether the damage was purposeful or not. What matters is..." Her face winced as her mind strained into what looked like a headache. She pressed on, "how my people react."

Lowering her elbows onto the table and bowing her head, the queen closed her eyes and fell silent.

"If we try to place a statement now, it could resolve the shock," Isaac suggested.

"Or it can look like we're just saving face," I countered. "I'm more worried about what Unfortunates will think. This paper can sway more to join the AGM."

"You expect Unfortunates to do what? Read?" Minister Gabriel scoffed. "I doubt their Gifted Houses will share such vile words out loud, much less to their servants."

"Not all Unfortunates are servants, minister," I clarified.

Minister Gabriel turned to me slowly and spoke decisively. "And every day, more servants deny themselves forgiveness when they turn away from their Gifted House."

I swallowed hard. If Melanie's life wasn't in danger, I would tear into him, but I needed to save my energy.

"If the Anti-Gifteds Movement is capable of writing," I

spoke smoothly, "they're very well capable of reading too. And sharing with those who are willing to listen."

Silence enveloped the meeting room as we all reflected on our best course of action. Queen Maya remained still, concentrated, until she opened her eyes and stood upright.

"We have little to no information on this newspaper. Have City Guards and extra Royal Crest Knights in Unfortunate cities. I want another taskforce looking into the AGM and examine the package drop off patterns if possible. Are there any palace servants or staff missing?"

"None missing, ma'am," Isaac replied.

The queen sighed. "That's a relief. Assemble Royal Crest Knights, third year, and second year Galdor students to begin patrols along smaller villages and ghost towns where the AGM or Diviner can be hiding. Norburn is a dead end right now."

Including second years was stretching our military thin. It would also be the perfect means of sneaking out if we faked a mission like we did to find the Diviner before we knew his identity. But I refused to drag my classmates through another slaughter. I couldn't afford another Norburn incident; another needless death.

Queen Maya dismissed the meeting, and both Isaac Winters and Minister Gabriel went about their new tasks. I needed to remove myself from the queen's side to finally ensure Melanie was safe. She wouldn't let go without a good excuse.

Mercy greeted us outside the Senior Circle meeting room, pacing herself in front of the queen whereas I fell behind. Here was my chance.

Stuffing my fingers down my throat, I gagged. Chunks from breakfast fell from my mouth and onto the polished marble floor. Silently, I apologized to the Unfortunate who would clean up after me.

Queen Maya gasped. I continued to cough, hunched over, and hoping that my face appeared pained and sickly.

"Mercy, take her to the infirmary."

Mercy nodded, gently placing a hand on my shoulder.

"I'm fine." I sloppily wiped off the vomit from my lips.

"Take her to the infirmary," the queen repeated, "I need you at your best."

"Your Majesty," I mumbled, my gait purposefully uneven as I stepped.

First phase complete.

As we entered the infirmary, I looked for Mr. Harris in each cot we passed. I didn't find him.

"I hope you get better," said Mercy as she waved off. "See you soon."

The nurse checked my forehead and throat. Finding nothing, I played along until she concluded that it must be a stomach bug. I agreed with her diagnosis, pretending my body was too frail to leave. My head rested on the pillow but I did not rest.

Even in all my pretending, I couldn't push my friends away.

Fern came in, trying to offer me a cookie that Kai said I didn't need in my state. Persephone and Leo came in together, followed by Skylar.

"What are you doing here?" I forced a whisper.

"We came to see you!" Fern chirped.

"I just wanted to see you in a weak state," Skylar quickly countered. "I also came to punch you in the face, but you look like shit already."

Good, I thought. My ruse was working. "Thanks," I replied flatly.

Kai stepped closer to the small cabinet near my bedside.

"May I look at your medical chart?" he asked.

I wanted to say no because he would find nothing but outright refusing him would also be suspicious. "Nurse says it's a stomach bug" I said. "I should be fine by tomorrow. Just need plenty of rest."

He lingered there but didn't pick up the clipboard.

"Sleeping on the job is the best," Leo winked.

My heart quickened in panic. Did he see through me?

Persephone rolled her eyes, "Like you could use any more sleep."

No, just banter. My face pressed deeper into the pillow.

Fern came closer, "Have you heard about the AGM newspaper yet? They're calling it the Divine…what again?"

"The Divine Observer," reminded Kai.

I nodded but refused to indulge. I needed to change the subject, my mind still on Melanie.

"Where's Molly?" I prompted.

"She's doing a bit of 'resting' herself," said Skylar, exaggerating 'resting' with air quotes.

Persephone gave the Aura a side glance before adding, "She's not doing well. I think you need to talk to her. She doesn't have anyone else."

I thought about those words. How her parents rejected her now that she was an Unfortunate. How she rejected herself not long after. Could I really be the only one who knew her well enough to say something that mattered? Regardless, I knew I couldn't talk to her now. I couldn't tell her that her sister was in danger or how I knew.

"I will tomorrow," I said, fully aware that I could be nowhere near Galdor tomorrow. He would see me soon. "Thank you for checking on me."

Second phase complete.

⁎

As night fell, I reached for my ID at my bedside and fumbled around in search of it. I sighed as the card finally reached my fingertips. There was no way for me to assign myself a patrol the way I had last time. No prince arrived to help me like he had.

No, this time, I had to scale the 12-foot wall that protected the Iridion Castle and Galdor Academy. A seemingly impossible task—but I needed to do it.

Running through the night was too familiar. Cloaked in darkness, I stuck to the shadows like second nature. Sylvia Douglas was right: I would make a good AGM member.

That was a strange thought. I shook it away, focusing on the ever-growing wall in front of me. There were four watchtowers. My best bet was the bottom right corner of the wall that intersected the east and southern sides.

Running past the servant quarters, I stared up at the wall and it stared back in imposing silence.

As my hand touched the brick, I heard a yelling,

"HEY!"

I flinched, retreating my hand back towards my chest and sharply turning to my right. A silhouette of a guard stood offensively in the mid distance, his flashlight illuminating my face.

Dammit.

Usually, the south tower didn't pay attention so closely to the servant section of the compound. But with the Anti-Gifteds Movement growing more dangerous, so were the Gifteds who monitored them.

I pulled on my sleeve to hide my brand as I raised my hands

up in an appeasing gesture.

"Approach!" he ordered. "Slowly!"

I did; we met at the middle between the corner of the wall and the south watchtower.

He noticed my academy combat attire, and I noticed the three stripes on his jacket denoting him as a third year.

"What are you doing?" he demanded.

"Nothing of interest, sir." Years of practice held my polite voice.

"Why are you in your combat uniform this time of night?"

"I'm going on a solo mission, sir," I lied. It was the quickest lie I could muster, and I regretted it immediately.

He squinted. "Then why are you here and not at the entrance?"

I fumbled on my words, "I'm making my way over there. I just like to...take a walk the long way round the Grounds before every dispatch."

Could I be so lame? I stared at him, hoping he would somehow buy into the ridiculousness of my explanation.

His squint remained. "Then you won't mind if I confirm your mission."

His hand reached out. My heart pounded in my chest. I couldn't refuse him and get away now.

"Not at all, sir," I forced.

Slowly, I handed my ID to him, trying my best to keep my arms steady to avoid suspicion. There was nothing on this ID. No way for me to fabricate a patrol. He would soon find out I was lying. Third phase failure.

He spoke my information over the walkie talkie on his chest, relaying back to the south watchtower. We waited in painful silence. Counting my heartbeats became impossible. How long had it been since he requested confirmation? I kept my eyes lowered.

Static sliced through the air, "The rest of her team is waiting at the front gate, over."

My eyes widened in surprise, and the man held a similar reaction staring at me. "I thought you said you were going on a solo mission."

Revealing my shock worked in my favor. I snatched my ID from his hand. "I thought so too. Guess I shouldn't keep them waiting on me."

His suspicion didn't end there though as he begrudgingly walked me towards the front entrance gate on the west side of Galdor.

Kai's form appeared first out of the shadows, twirling his ID in his hands.

"There you are!" he shouted. The rest of my classmates surrounded him, and that was enough for my escort to back off.

My heartbeat didn't slow as I approached my team. More frantic questions cluttered my mind as the front gates opened, and we walked through without incident.

After several minutes of silence and a considerable distance away from any ears, I finally spoke. "How did you know—?"

"Nothing in your chart suggested illness, you asked about Molly out of nowhere, and Melanie was reported missing by her parents this afternoon."

Kai spilled out his words as if he'd been holding on to them for much longer than he liked.

He pressed on, "So how did *you* know Nora? Before Molly did? Before any of us did? Even better, how do you know where to find her if you're so willing to go to these lengths to sneak out and then get caught?"

I choked on hesitation. I couldn't tell them.

"Yeah, and now that you're not sick," Skylar stepped forward, gaining pace, "let's make sure that you're not Ebony Nique!"

She punched me square in the face and I let her. Using her Gift behind the punch, I fell onto the concrete and stayed there. Gravel punctured my skin but I didn't care.

Looking up, Skylar huffed. "Well, that answers that question. Are you an AGM member then?"

"You know damn well I'm not!" My body flashed with heat. "I just—"

You tell them, and her Gift is mine.

My teeth gritted; I wanted to scream and couldn't even do that. "I was informed by Isaac—"

"The truth, Nora," Leo cut in.

The warehouse enclosed around me. Molly screamed as Cassius pressed his hand along her forehead. A red and black light ignited brighter than any fire and blinded me as her Gift tore away into his hand.

I needed to reach Melanie. I lied again, better this time.

"Isaac Winters *did* tell me at the Senior Circle meeting that Melanie was missing. He thought I should break the news to Molly but I also wanted to investigate first and hopefully save Molly from the same fear. Cherryville has a lot of distance between houses so...she could still be in the area. Just not where she's supposed to be. Satisfied?"

My teammates fell silent. Considered my lie. I prayed that they thought it true or at the very least just accepted it anyway. Tears cleaned the dirt from my face.

"Then let's find her together," said Fern.

"No!" I shouted. "I refuse to put you in danger again! Not like what happened in Norburn! I can't do that to you."

Especially with what I knew. I was walking into a trap, and

they were freely doing the same. I needed to go alone.

"Please, go back," I begged, "If we find the Diviner again—"

"Not a damned chance!" Molly's voice was filled with her past poison, pushing forward and her face darkened in shadow. "The Diviner took my Gift away. He does *not* get to do that to my sister. Now get up."

I stumbled to my feet immediately at the spark reignited in her body.

"We understand the risk and we're doing it anyway," noted Kai.

I shook my head, "*Why?*" Why were they doing this to me?

"Because you said it yourself," Fern lifted up my chin to meet her emerald eyes. "No one truly does anything alone."

She offered me a small smile of encouragement before walking past me. The rest of my teammates did too, some more hesitant than others. They were all afraid but moved forward regardless.

Hesitantly, I did the same. Walking together to the train station, I found myself relieved I wasn't going alone. But terror gripped my nerves about whatever was awaiting us in Cherryville.

CHAPTER TEN

Hidden in the Crawford House

An open and black sky greeted us as the train doors opened in Cherryville, the rural town expansive enough for stars to lightly direct our path. A far cry from the buzzing atmosphere in Galdor, the train station was at least not as run down as I could recall from Norburn. A few stragglers entered and exited the train car.

Molly pushed me to exit first.

"So this is where you're from, huh?" Fern turned to look at me.

My mouth stretched into a line, thinking about a family in Thunder Bay that didn't see me outside of the few coins in my pocket. "Yeah, I guess you can say that."

"We need to get moving." Molly was urgent, more urgent than I'd seen her in a long time.

Determination hardened her face, but spirals swirled in her

dull amber eyes. The more time we wasted, the more she unraveled.

Since houses were further apart and mostly empty during half the year, we had to walk the rest of the way. The Montgomery house was a 30-minute walk diagonally from the train station, which meant that the Crawford house was about the same in the opposite direction.

How was I supposed to convince them to reach the Crawfords without question—without exposing my connection to our leading enemy?

I tried reaching for Cassius in the back of my mind.

That icy feeling didn't run down my spine when his presence became known. His lack of communication only worked to torment me more. Melanie had to be at the Crawford house. He wouldn't have shown me otherwise.

As the train pulled away, I prompted Molly, "We should check the Crawford house first."

Kai raised an eyebrow and Leo squinted.

"Why's that, Nora?" Leo crossed his arms.

I continued to push, "She's not going to be home if she's *missing.*"

"No, no, no," Molly paced about. "We need to go see my parents first."

"And do what? Get information out of them they don't have?" I countered, old habits slipping into my tone with ease. "You know the Crawfords typically don't visit their home in winter. It'll be empty and perfect for the AGM."

Molly continued to pace, tugging at her hair, its hue no longer the color that heated her face.

"That's where I was heading when you caught me," I added. "It's the best start if you're still..."

I looked at the Gifteds around me. How could I lead them

into a trap like this? Fail them all over again? I needed to push them away, but I didn't.

"...willing to help." I finished.

"We are," replied Kai.

"I'm just here because I think Mr. Harris would come back from wherever he is just to kill me if you died," Skylar commented from the side. She glared at me, "And I'd hate to see a repeat of last time we snuck out like this."

That made two of us.

Trudging through the darkness, our collective silence left room for thoughts of you, Valerie.

We dreamed about escaping to a place like these rolling hills because we didn't know anything better. A little cottage where you baked and I cooked; where we could embrace each other without fear and work without obligation. We would keep the house clean because it was second nature, and we would find time to rest at days end. We would discover new hobbies and pursue them. We would scribble notes to each other for the fun of it, and we would hoard second-hand books when we found them. I always wanted to read to you the way you could sometimes—when you first arrived at the Montgomerys and were more educated than me.

I realized how free-form my thoughts were; how your presence filled and tore my heart with love and longing, and I silently thanked Cassius that he didn't interrupt.

The outline of the Crawford house came into view. Because the Crawfords often stayed in Cherryville in the winter and not almost year-round like the Montgomerys, I only made the journey maybe once, twice a year.

The Crawfords had three servants. One was the frantic younger servant worried about orange slices at Molly's acceptance party. Was that really a year ago? Did she, along with the others, join the AGM? Perhaps I would find out while we tried to kill each other.

All lights were snuffed out of the Crawford home.

We cautiously approached the door, foreboding threatening to paralyze me in place with each step. Turning the doorknob, the house opened with relative ease.

Darkness swallowed our vision. Even with the door wide open, we could only see the entrance hallway and the bottom of the staircase leading to the second floor. Recognizing the brass railings, I glued my feet to the ground. I couldn't carelessly run up the stairs. I couldn't create another Norburn incident.

A loud creak stretched out above us. We all snapped our necks upward to the second-floor railing that spanned the first-floor wall.

My heat beat louder in my chest. He could attack from the second floor all over again. And in a much closer space than a warehouse, we were bound to burn.

Molly remained at the entrance way, keeping a glimpse of hope that we could escape this time. The last time we encountered the Diviner, she didn't make it to the exit before he caught her.

The creaking above continued. Faster, quicker, running.

A dark ambiguous shape barreled towards me. I readied my sword.

Something collided and wrapped tightly around my hips.

"I got you!" Melanie squealed. Her giggle echoed through the empty house, but my heart continued to fill with dread. This was wrong.

Melanie chanted my almost name over and over again. I slowly bent down to meet her eye level.

"When are we going back home, Mora?" she whined, "Your

friends don't like playing."

I held my shaky hand out, trying my best to appear composed for her. "Where are my friends, sweetie?" I asked, "Can you see them?"

She peered into the darkness and pointed: the top of the staircase and the darkness to our immediate right. Gazing up to the second-floor balcony, Melanie frowned, "I don't know where the other one went."

The Gifteds around me tensed, all standing in defensive positions.

I swallowed hard, clinging onto Melanie's hand. "I'm going to need you to go with Molly, okay?"

Melanie started to whine, twisting her torso back and forth. I held onto her tighter, trying to remember how she felt now lest I never see her again.

"Miss Melanie," I started, "please go to your big sister."

"But I want *you*!"

"I'll be right behind you, miss."

"Do you promise?"

Large blue orbs stared impatiently at me. She could still see in the dark; her Lux Gift was still intact. Cassius kept true to his word. I could promise her anything.

"I promise."

Melanie's smile radiated from her face. She released her grip on me and sprinted toward Molly. The two sisters ran out of the house together.

I trained my eyes to the staircase. *Where are you? I wondered.*

An unnatural silence hung in the air. The wood shifted and creaked, mimicking the house resting.

Maybe we shouldn't find out.

Metal sliced through the air. With a sharp wave of Kai's

fingers tightly compacted together, a thin layer of ice collided with the knife hurdling at Fern.

"It worked!" Kai's face switched to wonderment.

"You weren't sure!?" demanded Fern.

A flicker of motion brought my attention to the front door. I caught sight of Poppy's form and a new mallet in hand as the door slammed shut from the inside.

"No!" I screamed.

An inky blackness swallowed our sight. I stumbled back as I heard her race forward.

A large shadow cast overhead. As I rolled to the left, Poppy plunged her giant mallet into the floor. The wood paneling snapped and splintered apart, and the team jolted into action.

Fire ignited on the right side of my vision. Persephone's face illuminated briefly as her eyes fixated on the melting iron running down her palm. "There's two here!" she called.

Two AGM members revealed themselves from where Melanie pointed to. One kept her distance upstairs, confronting Fern and Kai. Skylar and the Mati twins attacked the other to my right.

I glided and stopped at the edge of a rug in the living room. Poppy stood to her full height. She turned in my direction, "You're already learning."

Her comment struck a nerve. "I don't need combat lessons from *you*!"

"Poppy?" Fern called out to the AGM Unfortunate.

Poppy turned her head and the two looked at each other with familiarity. Her lips stretched back into a smile. "I'll get to you in a moment, Miss Fairaway."

She adjusted the mallet in her hands and charged at me.

I stepped back as Poppy swung at me. Twisting the rug, Poppy twisted too far and faltered. I tripped her and pointed my sword down.

She cursed, swinging the mallet with one hand. My sword ricocheted and disappeared somewhere past the couch.

I sprinted after it. Before I could jump over the sofa, wood pressed against my neck as Poppy retaliated, her mallet horizontal to my throat. I held onto the sides with all my might as Poppy pulled me back to her.

Thrashing, I desperately clung onto any pockets of air as she suffocated me.

We stumbled, our heights uneven. I stood on my heels, pushing us back far enough to fall over. Glass shattered as we fell through the coffee table.

I rolled out of Poppy's hold, small shards pressing into my palms as I stood. Wincing, I hastily pulled them out.

Poppy left her mallet on the ground and clutched my wrist.

Fern fiddled with small metal pieces as Kai covered her. Using the finite amount of water he carried with him, he formed a door-like shield that protected their bodies. Peering out, he kept his fingers flat and tightly together. Sharp fragments of ice retaliated like a blade. The AGM member pivoted along the second-floor landing.

"How is it going?" Kai called.

Fern curled her fingers and pulled away from her palm; the metal between her hands slowly stretched into a point.

"Almost done!" she called back.

The second AGM member deviated the Mati siblings but lost her footing as Skylar swept her up into the air. She slammed into the side wall. Her comrade gasped, running down the stairs to assist.

Poppy brought me close, stepped forward a few feet to avoid broken glass, and threw me back to the ground. She straddled me from behind, digging her knees into my elbows.

With both hands, she lifted my chin so I could look out in front of me.

"Done!" Fern stepped out and threw the needles at the AGM assailant. She yelped, hitting the bottom of the stairs hard near the hole Poppy intended for me.

With their backs arched and arms wielding different forces of nature, my teammates exhibited a malice I associated with other Gifteds as they stepped closer to the two Unfortunate girls. Eyes glanced about nervously.

You've imagined the way Valerie died, Cassius's voice reverberated in my Unfortunate soul. *Is this how you pictured it?*

I struggled beneath Poppy, fear seeping into my nerves.

"Stop!" I yelled. "Fern! Stop!"

She did; they all did. But in that moment of hesitation, the girl closest to Fern and Kai pulled out a circular metal object and ripped out its safety pin.

Persephone sprinted forward, enclosing the grenade with both hands.

Her knuckles lightened as she contained the blast within her fist. Heavy smoke seeped out between her fingers.

The AGM member against the wall screamed, throwing another grenade at Skylar and Leo.

Leo held out his hand, clenching into a fist as the bomb hurled toward them. It exploded pre-maturely from his command, but his good arm strained and failed to contain the impact.

Skylar gasped and stepped in front of his wounded arm, her palm out next to him. Shrapnel sprayed around them, redirected straight through the ceiling by the forcefully crafted wind.

Several pieces still broke through before the Aura could

defend, thinly cutting their shoulders, arms, and legs.

With no other means to escape, the closest AGM member at the staircase glanced in our direction. She looked at her commander for guidance, and Poppy nodded.

The two girls looked at each other the way Unfortunates did when something was deeply wrong but we kept our mouths shut anyway. It was the way you and I would say, *This world is cruel, but we have each other.*

Each took out a blade.

"Wait!" Persephone yelled.

She and Fern reached out first, but it was too late. Blood spewed from their chests like rain, and the two Unfortunates fell over almost effortlessly.

I shrieked, and Poppy released her hold. As I stood, a flash brightly captured the scene in front of me. I turned back in time to see my face contorted in the reflection of the lens.

"What do you think for the new issue?" Poppy spat. "I'm thinking 'Iridon's First Unfortunate Soldier Complicit in Two Unfortunate Murders.'"

My breaths became more rapid and irregular.

She tried to flee. A screech festered in my throat. I grabbed ahold of her. Poppy's serious demeanor darkened.

"You still want to catch me? What do you think happens next? I'll die too, and you'll have no one to blame but yourself!"

Flinching, my hands released her easily. Sylvia Douglas hung from the flag post. All because of me. All because I was a traitor to my own people. I couldn't bring another Unfortunate to the same fate.

She ran out the back door; I grabbed my sword and retreated back to my friends.

"We're just going to let her get away?" Skylar demanded.

I didn't look at her. "We got what we came for."

I trudged outside where the night greeted me. The Gifteds followed in silence. I caught sight of Molly and Melanie far off near the road. Headed toward them, a bright fire festered within me.

Another Norburn incident didn't happen. He wasn't here like I expected.

So *why*—why were tears streaming down my face? Why did my heart burn and why did my throat swell so tightly I couldn't breathe?

I prayed for rain to quench me.

CHAPTER ELEVEN

Property Returns to Montgomery House

———

Rain fell from Molly's face. She held her younger sister, relief overtaking her usual despondent expression.

I stared for too long at the new sight.

On replay, the two Unfortunate girls died within my memory. Even if this was Cassius's doing, I didn't want to forget either.

Fern wrapped her arms around her chest and held her hands right below her chin. I approached but couldn't bring myself to hold her. I brushed her side instead.

"I'm calling the ERS. It's best we leave before they arrive," Kai finally broke the silence.

"They're not alive, Kai," Leo replied dryly.

"No, but they should be recovered."

"We need to take her to my parents," suggested Molly, "before we head back to Galdor."

My voice snapped, "Are you crazy? You're lucky she's alive! We just— I—" As I stepped forward, Melanie flinched and sank further into her sister's embrace.

Anger continued to boil my blood as I tried a lower pitch. "Let the responders take her back. I'm..."

Breaking.

"...asking."

"No!" Molly didn't give up, swallowing hard through sobs. "I came all this way for her. She's not leaving our sight until she's *home.*"

My fingers curled inward. I didn't want to go back to the Montgomery house, but I couldn't leave Molly to walk that hour by herself either. And I couldn't allow the others to return early because we'd be missing members. That would alert Isaac of our transgression if he wasn't already suspicious.

"We don't have time to argue," I caved. "You and I will take Melanie, and everyone else can head to the train station. We can meet up there and arrive back to Galdor together. Is that to your satisfaction, Molly?"

Against my best efforts, despondency still laced my words. The Diviner was building a formidable Unfortunate army. One that could withstand Gifteds and one that was willing to kill and die instead of accepting defeat. He grew in strength with each passing move of a game I couldn't fully understand. How many would he recruit with one photograph?

Skylar glared at the child. "How do we know the little brat isn't Ebony Nique?"

"Skylar," I warned.

"It's a valid question!"

"Well, you're not punching her in the face to find out."

Skylar squinted. "It's just awfully suspicious for her to be so unscathed and come right to us unharmed. She was even in a house of AGM members and they didn't torment her?"

As Skylar stepped forward, I found enough energy to obscure Melanie's form. Molly held her sister tighter, turning her away from the brewing conflict.

"Cassius wouldn't do that to her." I stopped myself from saying *"He kept his promise"*. Immediate regret swirled in my heart as Skylar's expression tightened and her eyes resembled that of a shark's again.

"*Cassius?*" she hissed. "What do you know about Cassius and what he would or wouldn't do?"

I stepped back as Skylar slinked forward.

She continued, "Don't tell me you're still *fawning* over him, forgetting entirely what he truly is. A deserting prince who thinks himself Divine justice. A Gift stealer and killer."

Her breaths grated through gritted teeth, so close to my face I could feel the warmth. What was happening to us? We were back to when she first learned I was an Unfortunate and not when we worked together as a team.

"We're not doing this," I finally said, adding space between us. "We're not letting him get to us. I know she's not Ebony because I would recognize the girl *I* raised."

"You really do consider yourself an exception."

"Well if she kills us on the way back to the Montgomerys, you can be satisfied in being right."

I turned away from her and ended the confrontation there. We parted.

Melanie stood between us, holding each of us by the hand.

Our bodies already tired from the fight and adrenaline left behind several miles back, Molly and I walked over an hour to the Montgomery house.

Its presence greeted me with sickly familiarity. I recognized the patch of discolored brick, the flowers pressed against the house perimeter—the way they sprouted and colored and danced—and the glass door panel right before the front one.

Molly reached for the doorknob, but I raised my hand and knocked quickly instead. She retracted, and we waited.

The door opened; Mrs. Montgomery came into full view. Surprised, I couldn't help how my eyes widened. Where was the replacement servant to greet us? Had they not replaced me as expected?

She crossed her arms and raised her nose. "It's the middle of the night. What are you doing here?"

My lips twitched but words failed to form. She looked at me expectantly.

"We found Melanie," Molly finally said, lifting her hand up as proof.

Relief washed over Mrs. Montgomery's face until she caught sight of Molly's brand and her smile instantly faded. Molly noticed, trying to turn her palm away.

"Mama, Mora is back!" Melanie chirped up. She jiggled my arm, and I was thankful she was holding me by my unmarked hand.

Mrs. Montgomery's voice remained dry, "Yes, I see that. Thank you, Melanie." Her blank eyes met mine, "Does she have her Gift?"

I forced my eyes to remain on her. The real question was, *"Is she still above you?"*.

"Yes, ma'am," I nodded.

Mrs. Montgomery's face softened. Her lips parted like she intended to speak but even her breath held. Slowly, she clutched the fabric at her chest and bent her head down.

"Thank the Divine," she whispered.

After several shaky breaths, Mrs. Montgomery inhaled and straightened her posture back to vacant disdain.

"I see you haven't forgotten your manners. I'm not taking you back, though."

I squinted and responded slowly. "I'm not asking for my job back."

"Good. Melanie, let's come inside. These two need to head on their way."

"What?" Molly dropped her sister's hand.

"That's right. If you want thanks for bringing my daughter back, great, here you is your thanks, but no Unfortunate is allowed in my house again. Melanie, come now."

The glass cover opened just wide enough for the child to squeeze through. My hand was left cold from her quick departure.

Before Mrs. Montgomery could shut us away, Molly managed to wedge her foot into the door and keep it ajar for a heartbeat longer.

"You still treat me as you do *her*!?" Molly tossed her arm to gesture at me. "I just saved my sister from the AGM!"

Mrs. Montgomery's arm swung back, her open palm arched. Molly flinched and stumbled back; my posture straightened and my jaw tightened waiting for impact.

But Mrs. Montgomery stopped herself mid-way, hesitation swelling in her eyes.

Her voice trembled, "It's time you learned your place and find redemption elsewhere. She is no longer any concern of yours. And for all I know," Mrs. Montgomery regained her stern posture and pointed an accusing finger in my direction, "*she* is in the AGM. How else would they know where to find her?"

"I'm still considered your property, Mrs. Montgomery."

"That's right, and I have to watch you both plague this family on the news over and over again. It's disgusting. Now get away from my house or I'll have both of you arrested."

The door slammed shut in Molly's face.

Her jaw tightened, and her body shook as something dark pent up inside her. She clutched her right hand with her left, hiding the scar there. Weeps replaced words as Molly stood at her own front door and couldn't enter.

It was difficult to imagine there was ever a time I feared her.

I reached out, "Molly..."

She smacked my hand away and turned to me, her face red and hot and human. "I won't be comforted by an *Unfortunate*."

I forced my eyes to stare into hers that no longer trained on me like prey. Mustering the most sincere voice, I said, "Melanie still loves you. She doesn't know the difference."

"*Shut. Up!*" Molly pushed me to the side, baring her teeth like she still had fangs. She realized too, her mouth slowly closing and tightening. She swallowed hard. "She's home. That's all. I'm going."

I stayed at the front door for several heartbeats, watching Molly walk along a knife's edge between who she had been and who she was now.

She found her place at the back of the group and in the train car's corner on the way back to Galdor.

Giftless.

Sisterless.

Alone.

CHAPTER TWELVE

Black Box II

———

When we arrived back to Galdor Academy, re-entry was more seamless than the last time we snuck out under false pretenses.

Everyone was accounted for, and we were checked into the infirmary for inspection rather than necessity. And even though I never wanted to see Mr. Harris look at me with such anger and disappointment as he did after the Norburn disaster, I didn't realize how much I wanted him to look at me at all.

I needed his guidance. Skylar grew more temperamental to Leo. Any excuse for an argument became a production as if the two knew they were supposed to fight and did so to keep themselves separated. Kai started eyeing me without concealment. Every movement I made was analyzed by his stare, and it forced me to over-analyze each action even down to how I held a spoon, who I looked at while speaking, and how long I stood completely still.

And Molly... I hadn't seen her since we returned from her old house. Persephone asked me to talk to her. But what was I supposed to say to someone who hated me and hated herself because she hated me?

Even worse, I looked at the rankings this morning and found that Molly slipped to the bottom. The very bottom, even below me. How could I possibly comfort her—or any of my team members when it was so clear that we were going in circles?

At least I could rely on Fern. She knew how to boost morale, especially when I couldn't.

But none of us were prepared for Isaac Winter's fury.

A few days after we snuck out, Isaac issued a Simulation Lab on our daily assignments. Molly showed up to my surprise, her arms crossed and eyes permanently downward.

A tower stood before us. Dense rain surrounded the building, and Isaac didn't brief us on anything until we reached the top on the tenth floor through the elevator oddly placed straight through the center. We watched him press the ground floor button, and the elevator fell back down to Level 1. The elevator shaft remained open and exposed.

Isaac finally spoke, "Your mission is to reach the first floor and leave the building."

Silence swept through the chilled space.

I concentrated on Gifted stares as they looked at our instructor expectantly. Rain continued to thud against the window pane, demanding my attention.

Kai's face scrunched. "That's it?"

"Yes," Isaac nodded, "I think I made myself quite clear."

"You just want us to leave?"

"Yes."

"No criminal Gifteds to arrest?" Leo prompted.

"Or assailants to attack?" Persephone added.

"No," Isaac clarified. "The only person you have to get past is me."

"All of us against you?" I asked.

"Yes, and this will also count as your combat exam for the year so take this seriously." Isaac remained unfazed. "I will be somewhere in the building and will change locations by the elevator shaft here. You are not allowed to use the elevator during this simulation." He pressed his hand firmly against the button and froze it over. "I'll catch you regardless."

Isaac entered the opening where the elevator used to be, each step forming an ice platform. He turned back to us, his tone as cold as his Gift.

"And if you *ever* sneak out under my name again, I will terminate you from Galdor Academy. Mr. Harris didn't when he had the chance, but I won't hesitate. Dismissed."

He dropped downward. No sound reflected back to us, giving us no indication of his whereabouts.

Leo scoffed. "He found out anyway after we were so careful."

Kai pressed his hand to his forehead in deep thought.

Skylar shook her head. "He wants us to fight him for our combat exam? I was looking forward to..."

Her eyes clocked onto my cheek. I grabbed her fist before she could punch me. With all this practice, my accuracy grew better and better with each passing day.

"You already tested my identity this morning, Skylar," I reminded her.

"*Besides*," Leo butted in, "don't want to lose points for teamwork, do you? I might surpass you after this simulation."

"Over my dead—"

"Stop!" I cut her off before they spiraled into another

argument. "Let's focus. Both of you are bound to lose points if you fight during a simulation. Are you two capable of working as a team?"

The two bristled at the word '*team*' and repelled from each other. I guess not.

As I sighed, an arm brushed my shoulder. Fern stepped next to me with more patience than I could muster myself. She couldn't possibly know that when Valerie did that, it meant *I'm here*, but my heart didn't discern as it fluttered.

Giving her an assuring smile, I looked at our surroundings. The floor was a completely empty space safe for the elevator at the center. An opening for a staircase resided on our right side but not on the left as our only exit downward.

I approached and peered, the descend darkened without any light source. If only we still had Molly's infrared sight.

"Who's going first?" Kai asked.

I half expected Fern to push him forward and volunteer him in an excited chirp. But her fingers interlocked with mine instead, freezing me in place before Isaac could make an appearance.

"It's best not to go alone, yeah?" she asked.

Our hands were still intertwined.

In my hesitation, Fern tilted her head. "Nora?"

I stammered, "Yeah, sure. Yes. Let's, let's go together. Kai?" I raised my other open palm for him to interlock too. His hand was cooler to the touch and smaller than Fern's.

"I'm not holding your hand," Skylar noted to Leo.

Leo laughed, "I don't need to." He leaned into his sister and grabbed her hand.

Molly silently charged forward and passed us, descending into the darkness by herself.

"Molly, wait!" I followed her, my teammates cascading

closely behind.

We all stepped back into the open on the next floor. A 9 was painted on the wall between two windows. Molly kept charging forward without care toward the staircase at the opposite side of the room; I pulled away from Fern and Kai to reach her.

Reaching the 8th floor where the layout of the top floor repeated itself, I finally caught her. Molly halted but didn't retract.

"We're supposed to work as a team," I said.

"Do it without me," Molly released herself from my hold. "I want this over with."

She crossed the empty space. We progressed to Level 7, saw the stairs at the other side, and began crossing again.

Nearing the next exit, the hair along my neck prickled.

A crash erupted behind me.

"Persy!" Leo called.

Trapped in a large sheet of ice, Persephone looked out from her prison with unblinking dismay. A flame ignited in Leo's palm.

Isaac flattened his hand and held his fingers tightly together. He made a slicing motion downward, and a wall of ice tore away from Persephone's confinement.

Sliding on the frosted ground with ease, Isaac used the momentum to push the block at Leo and Skylar. They both put their hands up, but their Gifts weren't fast enough as the block pushed them all the way back across the room and into the stairway for Level 8.

The ice began to crawl and attach itself to the wall's foundation. Leo ignited a powerful blaze and Skylar concentrated his flame.

A yellow light illuminated from Persephone as she tried to

melt herself out from the inside, too. Isaac stepped forward to reinforce her binds when Kai and I blocked him.

Isaac twisted a piece of ice in his right hand as it formed a handle. Bringing his fists together, he extended his left hand outward. Ice sculpted into a blade from the hilt, reflecting my own weapon.

He collided with me first; my feet pushed back from his force.

Parry, Cassius's voice instructed me.

I did what he asked on instinct, making sure to dodge to the side instead of back. *Lunge.*

I did, extending my body and returning in one smooth motion when I missed. Isaac managed to keep Kai at bay too, fending off his water whip.

You're training me while I'm awake now? I couldn't help but ask.

I need my brightest Unfortunate at her best, he replied.

I fumbled at the sound of my nickname.

Isaac lunged directly at my chest; I gasped and tensed for impact. The coil of Kai's whip wrapped around Isaac's blade, halting his action in place. Where the hilt and the whip met began to melt back to water from Kai's touch.

Both Mares gawked at the sight. Fern jumped forward while Isaac was distracted and brought the dirt around his feet upwards, surrounding him in a dome.

For a heartbeat, silence enveloped the room and I thought we trapped him well. But the earth cracked under the weight of heavy ice and broke open.

Red brightening his face, Isaac brought his palms together and inhaled sharply. When he separated his hands in a swooping down motion, ice spiked in all directions directly in front of him—directly at Kai and Persephone.

Two consecutive buzzing sounds erupted from above, telling us that they were defeated. But the simulation didn't end as it usually did under Mr. Harris's instruction.

Isaac turned to our direction, ice wrapping around his arms.

We ran down the stairs to the seventh level.

"Fern, wall!" I ordered.

Raising her hands up, the earth in front of her lifted and blocked the staircase leading upward. The dirt covering revealed a firmer base.

Fern scoffed, "Metal. Great. If I can peel back the floor, we can get to the first floor a lot faster."

"Great." The hair on my arms prickled. He was closing in. "Let's try that on a lower floor. He's right behind us."

Fern and I turned to run, but Molly sat down on the floor, looking at us with a blank expression.

"What are you doing?" I asked.

"Sitting."

My mouth twitched, "Sit? You're *sitting*? Isaac will freeze you."

"Good. Then I can leave."

I spoke faster, irritable. "Molly, I have never been more serious in my life. You might get kicked out of Galdor if your scores don't improve."

"I don't care."

"Where would you go?"

Molly's glare sliced through the air, "I. don't. care."

Fern jumped from her heels to her toes and back again in a nervous tick. She turned to her blockade, and her eyes widened. "We have to keep moving."

I turned too and saw the ice forming along the wall frame.

Looking back at Molly, she glumly returned my gaze.

"You know what?" I shook my head. "I'm not moving either."

"What?" Molly stood, disbelief overcoming her despondence.

I crossed my arms and raised my nose. "Yep. I'm not leaving you behind."

Molly's nose wrinkled, and she exposed her human teeth. "You're so stupid."

"And you're not thinking things through," I countered. "You're wasting yourself. I want to talk to you after this. You're not escaping me so easily."

"Fern," I turned to the Avlis, "no need for you to freeze with us. Get to the first floor, and—"

The blockade collapsed into large chunks; ice continued to crawl along the building's foundation as Isaac stepped down to our floor. He jolted his arms down, and the ice bands around his forearms shifted into multiple spikes.

"Try to bend metal while you're at it," I finished, my words quickening as fast as my heart beat. "I believe in you."

"How about—" Fern stepped closer to us and kept her attention on Isaac "—you believe in me *now*?"

Lifting her arms wide, the earth moved to her will and pushed to either side of us. We sank, and my palms hit the metal bottom. Fern stomped her feet flat onto the cool surface, reared back, and punched downward as hard as she could.

The metal split apart but didn't break.

Isaac sliced through her initial defense and frost hardened the ground around us. I couldn't unsheathe my sword so closely pressed to Molly and Fern. A staff formed around Isaac's fingers, extending into a scythe. He approached.

"Fern! Get out of here!"

"Just one," the Avlis reared back, "more!"

Isaac swung for our heads; we fell straight through to the next floor down. Landing on my side, all the air knocked out of my lungs and I couldn't move. A cascade of dirt filled my senses.

Fern sprung up, reaching her arms out to the hole. Her arms shook violently as she tried to curl the metal back to its original state. One piece slowly followed her command until it iced over from Isaac's Gift.

"Let's go," Fern stopped her futile mission and pulled me up.

"Molly!" I urged her forward. "Come on."

Clenching her fists, the Gifted-turned-Unfortunate screamed at me, "*Why do you care so fucking much?*"

Glass fractured into shards as the windows around us imploded.

Fern shielded me first. But the shield crumpled as a loud, piercing cry escaped her voice. I turned in time to see Fern fall to her knees and struggle to steady herself there. I supported her side as she tilted over, the earth rippling under her back as she shook violently.

"I got you," I repeated over and over again. A large piece of glass protruded out of her body, and blood dripped down the back of her leg.

"I'm," she strained to hoist herself up by her arm and then admitted, "*not* fine."

Rain turned to slush as it pooled into the fifth floor. Molly huffed and panted, looking at the glass that tore at her skin.

"It's okay," I brought myself closer for support, "we'll get you back to the infirmary and—"

"No." She instinctually tried pushing me away and then stopped herself in the process. She looked at me for several heartbeats and calmed her voice, "Okay."

Leo escaped from underneath the slush, gasping for air.

I looked at him puzzled, "How did you get here?"

"What was that, Leo?" Molly demanded.

He ignored us, looking back where he came from and reaching in. Skylar didn't protest, her eyes closed and arms locked inward, shivering. She fell into Leo; they blinked at each other. So they *were* capable of acting as a team.

Alarmed, Skylar instinctually pushed him back but lost her balance in the process. He watched her fall awkwardly back into the wet snow and didn't hide the snarky smile that came with her ridiculousness. I sighed. They could be a team for a moment at least.

"Simulation over."

We all swerved our eyes to the entrance way of the elevator shaft and saw Isaac leaning on the doorframe, its entire casing frosted over in a blue hue.

Simulation? I looked back to Fern. Her pain and her blood appeared too real. I had completely forgotten that she was actually fine, wearing a suit that reflected her injury. She must have forgotten too as the worried hopefulness swirling in her eyes changed to embarrassment with the realization.

I turned to Isaac, "But we're not done for yet."

Our instructor scoffed, "Nora, you can't always fight your way out of a situation. Understanding when to fight and when to flee will be critical when you want to fight again. Look at your teammates and tell me what you choose."

I did: Leo and Skylar were dampened from the wet ice and catching their breath from falling through a window. No doubt Isaac had a hand in the collision, forcing the two back into the building. Molly pressed herself against the wall between the two broken windows, panting and sobbing to herself in a frantic state I wanted to save her from. And Fern, though unharmed, still could feel the glass in her leg as though it was real and couldn't move as a result.

"Would you give us the chance to flee?" I asked.

Isaac's face remained stern, "No."

I stood, "That's not fair!"

"Look who's finally catching on!" Isaac matched my volume, ice spiking around his feet. "This is *at least* the second time you've sneaked out of Galdor and put your team in direct danger."

"We chose to go with her," Fern cut in.

"That's not the *point*, Fairaway," Isaac snapped. He kept his glare at me, "If you were smart and had fled from me when you had the chance, you wouldn't have found yourself in a no-win scenario."

He was right. He was right, and I was angry. Even in Cherryville, we could have taken Melanie and ran. I didn't have to stay, waiting for our demise. There was a moment when I realized that fact, but I hesitated.

"Then I have to live with the consequences," I countered. "I'm not backing down. The others can flee, and you can take me."

Frost clouded the air as Isaac sighed, "Still so careless. There's no guarantee—"

He flung his arm out at Leo and Skylar's direction. She gasped, pushing Leo out of the slush as it lifted and trapped her legs. She pulled to no avail as ice crawled up her hips, torso, arms...

Beep. Eliminated.

Isaac raced at Leo, "—that your friends will be spared too!"

Leo punched the air but fire didn't ignite from his cold, wet hands. Isaac closed the distance and grabbed onto the Mati's fist. Ice encased his arm; Leo dropped forward from the sudden weight. Lifting his hands up, ice formed upwards in sharp spikes and held Leo there on the ground.

Beep.

Molly didn't put up any fight, only bracing herself as sludge washed over her entire body.

Beep.

He stepped closer to me. Shakily, I unsheathed my sword, my fingers already burning from the cold's growing intensity. My unsteady breaths revealed themselves in smoke as the air sharpened in ice fragments.

Isaac lowered and bent down—the floor, the ceiling, the walls all turning blue.

"You're going to freeze to death," he explained, "or at least feel the effects as though you really are. And you get to watch everyone you care about fall to the same fate because of you. Simulation over."

My heartbeats matched the rhythm of the outside rain, pounding louder and louder.

Nora! The sword fell out of my hands, but I didn't hear it crash. I heard him though, so clearly, so alarmed, so fearful. He sounded like my Cassius.

Isaac blurred, titled, and vanished. The cold numbed and fell away. We didn't even make it halfway through the building.

Standing in his private training room again, I huffed a deep sigh. I didn't want to be here.

"Would you prefer a ballroom?" Cassius outreached his hand. Gifts swirled violently within beads and reflected all colors into our eyes.

"Is that how you see Gifteds?" I asked.

He twisted his wrist, revealing greens and browns and yellows. "Beautiful, isn't it?"

So bright, my eyes remained wide and mesmerized. "Which one...is mine?"

A puzzled expression crossed his face, "None of these are yours. Your light is..." He stepped closer, "different than what I know from Gifteds or Unfortunates."

My fingers loosely curled around the sword's hilt, but my muscles ached and threatened to tear me apart. I remained still and stared at all shades of blue colliding in his gaze.

He drew closer. "A Gift is supposed to reside here." He pressed a gentle finger on my chest and where my heart started.

"And then it," he drew a curving line along my collarbone, up my neck, my jawline. His hand found my cheek and lingered there; his thumb rested at the edge of my lips, "breathes life through the rest of your body."

I inhaled slowly, "But I'm not a Gifted."

"No." His voice was so quiet and yet filled my entire senses. "No, you're something much greater. Something I can't explain and someone so incredibly bright."

My blade pointed downward like dead weight. I couldn't bring myself to lift it. I couldn't bring myself to fight him.

Not when he stared at me with that pained expression. The same pain when he said he wanted me by his side.

"Why do you keep doing this?" I whimpered.

His eyes lowered. "You still choose her."

"This isn't about your sister. I made a promise, Cassius."

"Yes, whatever the cost. But you're not willing to uphold all that promise entails. You don't realize how..." his hold desperately tightened as he inhaled, "how important you can be."

I pressed my hand over his, and he relaxed.

He continued, "We hold the same goal, Nora. I want to unravel you from this falsehood you insist on remaining allegiant to. They can't help you achieve our goal."

Cassius exhaled, "But you still deny me."

He pulled away, and I forced myself to remain still. "So as much as this pains me, I will respect your choice."

# CHAPTER THIRTEEN

How to Kill a Snake

Bright lights blinded my vision as I awoke. The white walls of the infirmary mocked me in their fake polish. Cassius's touch still lingered on my cheek.

Chatter became conversation around me. Fern and Kai sat facing each other; Persephone was still asleep underneath two blankets; Leo sat on his own bed without any blanket and faced Fern and Kai; Skylar finished requesting something from the nurse; Molly was missing.

"Morning, Nora," Leo called out, noticing me first.

"Is it really morning?" I lifted myself up in alarm.

"No, no," Leo laughed. "It's only been a couple hours."

Relief filled my sigh. I didn't have time to waste. "How are you guys holding up? Isaac was…" I trailed off. Before I could say 'ruthless,' everyone else filled in the space.

"Terrifying," said Fern.

"An asshole," Leo added.

"So cool," countered Kai.

We all looked to the Mare, but he studied his hands instead. "Did you see when I grabbed ahold of his sword? It melted."

Leo raised an eyebrow. "He's just not that into you."

"That's not even—the ice *melted* back into water." Kai turned to me, "Nora, you saw it right?"

I nodded. "Yeah. Doesn't that mean you're getting better at the ice side of your Gift?"

Kai tightened his lip in thought. "I don't think so. I've never managed to do that before. Hand me one of the warmer water bottles from Persy's bed."

"She needs those!" Leo protested.

"She can spare one." Kai walked over and grabbed one half-hanging out from her blanket cocoon. He walked back to his bed. "Warmer water freezes faster."

Leo folded his arms but didn't disagree.

We watched as Kai held the bottle and stared at still water inside. After what felt like a full minute, nothing happened and he gave up.

"I'll have to talk to Mr. Winters directly about this," he said.

Persephone groaned awake and adjusted in her cot. She looked around the infirmary, "Where's Molly?"

Skylar answered, "She and I woke up around the same time.

She just up and left without clearance but she didn't say where."

Persy swerved in my direction. "Did you not talk to her?"

"I..." Dazzling reds swirled along Cassius's wrists. I forced the dream away. I gripped my bedding like it was adequate evidence. "I haven't had *time*."

"You make time!" She sat up in her bed, heat radiating off her body. "*You're* the one who knows her best. *You're* the only one who knows what it's like to be an Unfortunate."

She pointed straight at my heart. Cassius pressed his finger in the same place. Standing out of bed, I jolted at the thought of him curving an outline up my body again.

"I'll talk to her soon," I stuttered. "I need, I need to see something first."

"What could be more important?!"

"Persy, you're going to give yourself a fever." Worry consumed Leo's face.

I left as the twins conversed. I would talk to Molly soon. I just needed to discern dream from reality before I unraveled.

I needed to know he wasn't in his personal training room. It was the same place where he first taught me how to protect myself. The same place where he first opened his true self to me—about his desire to prove himself more powerful despite his Makan Gift. We weren't so different then.

Swinging the training room door open, I wasn't alone. Molly stood on the other side in front of the weaponry, an ax in her hands.

The moment we recognized each other, Molly held the ax closer to her chest and fumbled on her words, "I didn't think anyone would come here."

"What are you...?" My brain was still processing what I was seeing. "Molly, why are you—?"

"I was hoping to do this in private," she interrupted. "Leave."

I swallowed hard and stammered, "I, I don't think I can." My body remained still but my face twitched relentlessly. Forming words became so difficult. "Molly, what are you doing?"

I knew perfectly well. I should have heeded Persephone's warning. Soon became now.

I stepped forward.

Molly's eyes widened; she lodged the ax between her collarbone and her throat. "Don't get any closer!"

I halted. My mouth dried; words scrambled too quickly in my mind to muster anything.

The ax shook between her fingers. "I refuse to be an Unfortunate anymore. And I refuse to die by any Unfortunate other than myself!"

"Molly," My voice barely registered over a whisper. Stepping forward a centimeter, I tried to get closer to her. Closer to the ax tucked under her chin. "I know you're hurting."

Tears puffed her face into a deep red hue and cracked her low voice, "You have no idea what it's like to have a Gift and then have it *ripped* away from you."

"No," I agreed, drifting forward. "But I have every idea what it's like to be an Unfortunate."

One step forward.

"I was powerful," Molly breathed. "Loved by my parents. Feared by you."

Second step.

"Respected enough to get here."

Third step.

"And then..." Molly's voice drifted. I was so close. If I

reached out, could I grab the ax in time?

She forced her words through the sniffles, "I was a coward."

Her hand slipped; I shouted and pulled the axe handle away.

She fought back with a desperate strength, blood trickling from the narrow incision in her neck.

"Stop!" she screamed. "I was a coward!"

We swung violently against the other, reminding me of my encounter with Poppy. Her features darkened in anger. "Let go! This is how you kill a snake!"

Distancing myself, I used our opposing grips to stabilize ourselves in place. The ax was positioned between us, too far away for Molly to use it against herself.

"I was downcasted! And it's"—her arms trembled—"all"—her fingers whitened—"my"—her grip loosened—"FAULT!"

We screamed as we collapsed, the ax in my possession. I quickly moved the blade away from my face but close to my chest, expecting Molly to attack me.

But she remained on the floor, her torso the only thing keeping her from completely lying down, from complete defeat.

"I..." Her chest rose and fell as she heaved. "...should have died with all the others. So why?"

She finally looked at me. "Why do *you* care so much?"

I stared into her eyes, those human eyes that once paralyzed me in place. She once picked me out in the rain, chose me as her property. She pushed me down the stairs, attacked the woman I loved, and tormented my life for *years.*

"You were a menace," I admitted, "but I don't think you deserve to die."

"I lost my Gift trying to keep it," Molly insisted. "I deserve to die."

"If you deserved to die, you should have like all the others," I refuted back.

Surprise softened her face at my harsh words.

I offered a small smile as I continued, "But since you are here, you can find redemption elsewhere."

I sat in a crossed position, placing the ax in my lap. "I'm here too, so we can figure it out together. Are you going to be okay with that?" I gestured to her wound.

She ran her hand along the mark and examined the blood. "It's not as deep as I intended," she said dryly.

I took that as a yes.

We stayed sitting awkwardly on the ground.

I watched her facial expression change in drastic waves as she wept. So many emotions I hadn't seen or ever seen plastered her face. I refused to take it away from her either. I was right here as promised.

As tears dripped to less and less droplets and her breathing regulated, she looked up at me—really looked into my Unfortunate soul. I looked right back.

In the softest voice I ever heard her speak, she uttered a small, "Thank you."

I inhaled slowly. "What are friends for?"

We stayed like that for a few minutes more until a knock reminded us of the outside world.

Molly tried to wipe away any remaining tears from her face and turned away from the door. I answered, instinctively hiding the ax behind my back.

Mercy leaned where the door opened; I fit myself into the small opening so she only saw me.

"Mercy!" I yelled her name in a fake excited greeting so Molly could hear. "What brings you to the training rooms?"

And the prince's personal one at that? I thought.

The Unfortunate placed her hands behind her back and straightened her posture. "Excuse the interruption, Miss Nora. Her Majesty requests your presence in the senior meeting room."

I squinted, this exchange all too familiar from when Sylvia Douglas knew my location. "And how did you know where I was, Mercy?" I asked.

"Intuition, ma'am," replied Mercy with expert precision.

"Intuition?" I repeated flatly.

"Yes, ma'am." Mercy pointed to her left. "It's my duty to know where you are at all times."

I can find you anywhere, Cassius said amidst an endless field of unity flowers, *especially through those who serve me.*

"Is it?"

Mercy blinked, "Yes, ma'am. The sovereign often requests for your audience in particular. We must hurry. There's been a development with the Anti-Gifteds Movement."

Suspicion shifted to alarm as she said those final words. "What development?"

"The newest newspaper, ma'am," Mercy clarified. "The Anti-Gifteds are framing the increasing number of downcastments as a punishment for anointing the wrong ruler."

This was not a conversation we needed to hear right now. I looked behind myself at Molly facing away from me. I couldn't abandon her.

I turned back to Mercy with a sympathetic look. "Please give Maya my apologies. I can't attend the meeting right now."

Mercy's eyebrows ruffled in confusion. Before I could close the door, she pressed inward and resisted. As I stopped, she did too, her eyes widening as she realized what she was doing. The Unfortunate stepped away and put her hands tightly behind her back again.

"Apologies, ma'am," she faltered. "This is of the highest priority. I cannot return to the queen without you."

"I'm sorry, but she can inform me of the details later," I urged. "I can't—"

"Unfortunates talking alone?" I saw Minister Gabriel's shadow before he appeared. "That doesn't bode very well."

"Minister," I begrudgingly acknowledged. He pushed through the door and entered the training room. I side stepped, all pleasantries removed from my voice. "Why are you here?"

"*Three* Unfortunates," he commented at the sight of Molly. She stood, face still swollen from tears. He noticed. "How far you've fallen, my dear."

"Leave her alone," I warned. "Why are you here?"

He looked at me with the same malice he portrayed at the Galdor Square massacre. "Why do you have an ax behind your back?"

My lips tightened. No answer, not even the truth, would alleviate the tension. I dropped the weapon; it clinkered to the ground.

"We were training," I replied.

"I see." Doubt laced his voice. "You got your opponent well with that primitive weapon. She should be in the infirmary."

Molly's eyes widened, and she covered her neck with her hand.

"We were just on our way," I lied.

"Make that now, then. I had to investigate why the queen's personal guard and personal servant weren't by her side. There isn't any AGM activity happening right now, is there?"

You would like that, wouldn't you? I thought. It would make his job so much easier getting rid of me.

"Of course not, minister."

"Then you won't have a problem separating yourself and attending to your queen."

I bit the inside of my cheek. He wasn't giving me a choice to decline. And the more he thought any of us were involved with the AGM, the more danger we were in.

"No, minister," I forced. "Molly, go check into the infirmary and check on the rest of team there, too."

There was no way I was leaving her alone to herself again.

Molly sheepishly nodded and quickly passed us. I watched her leave the facility and head in the right direction.

I turned to Minister Gabriel, forcing my face to appear as neutral as possible. "Shall we go to the Senior Circle together, minister?"

CHAPTER FOURTEEN

Time and Toll Escalate

Distracted during the Senior Circle meeting, all I gained was that the AGM newspaper pressured Gifteds to align their loyalty to the "correct" ruler—the Divinely chosen ruler—to escape downcastment. Stuffed into every mailbox and discussed in heated debate at every dinner table in Iridion, the AGM was now making an appeal to Gifteds to turn their loyalty.

Under the laws of Iridion, his Animus power was more than enough to determine him the rightful heir. But that fact was simply an introduction to his Makan Gift. What once ranked him barely above the status of an Unfortunate now ranked him above all others. That Gift he earned from birth. That Gift he earned from the Divine.

Unfortunates continued urging Unfortunates to join the Anti-Gifteds Movement. He united their front. He was their salvation.

The photo Poppy took of me wasn't in this issue, though.

Your image is being passed among AGM members instead, Cassius replied to my anxious thoughts. *To remind them of their fellow soldiers' sacrifice and to remind them of where you are.*

Where I am. Among Gifteds I deemed friends. Opposed to my own people.

Training days blurred as we were at the hem of Isaac Winters. He continued to push or punish us into better soldiers. Kai often worked alongside the Ice Mare, both getting used to Kai's ability to melt the ice Isaac created. Kai tried to explain it to me once in the past several sessions, but he talked about molecules and scientific jargon I couldn't quite wrap my head around.

I gathered: freezing water was difficult for most Mares—which was something Isaac could do with ease. Unfreezing water was difficult for Isaac—which was something Kai was learning to do with ease. Leo joked that they could complete the water cycle with his aid.

Molly and I started training together, too. She fiddled and fumbled with all different kinds of weapons, and we often sparred with wooden staffs. I caught myself recreating the fights against Cassius in my dreams or following his suggestions in my waking thoughts. Gifteds would fight us in rotation either one on one or both of us together.

Fire ignited in Persephone's hand during our most recent round of training. Molly trudged forward in the concealed Mati room, its environment replicating a desert setting. She dodged concentrated fire discs as they curved and spun, sinking and pulling herself out of the sand. I watched from the sidelines.

Persephone remained in place even as Molly gained ground. Molly lowered herself to evade another disc, close enough to grab Persephone in her next offensive. Molly tightened her fist and pushed herself up.

Sand sprayed everywhere as Molly suffocated Persephone's flame. But grains also got all over the Mati's face and eyes. She stumbled, her face scrunched and eyes tightly closed.

Molly stepped back with her hands over her mouth in a guilty expression, trying to hold back a chuckle. I didn't contain myself though, busting into laughter as the dust dissipated.

"I am so," Molly glanced at me and struggled to sound sincere, "not sorry, Persephone." A smile lightened her face as she giggled once. "I won!"

Sand still clung to Persephone's skin, but she could at least look at her perpetrator. Her smile broke any tension. She nodded. "You won."

Leo opened the exit door. "Food time, Pers!" he called to his sister. "You can stop eating the sand!"

He left the door open but walked away. Our other team members trailed from exhaustion. At least the second half of today would involve sitting down in developmental classes.

"Hey, I'm going to hang back with Persephone," I told Molly.

She waved us off and lumbered to the exit.

"What's up?" Persephone continued to dust herself out.

I rubbed my hand along my arm, my voice lowered even though we were right in front of each other.

"I just wanted to apologize for not talking to Molly when you warned me to. If I had, then maybe...I don't know. She wouldn't have to get herself out of such a steep hole."

Persephone's lips formed a line. "You don't need to apologize to me. I'm just glad she's here. Any one of us could have stepped up, but I could tell she needed you. Even if she especially thought otherwise."

"You weren't worried that I would be spiteful for all that time as her servant?" A genuine weariness hid behind my playful smile.

Persephone shook her head an immediately responded, "No. You lost any spite when Molly lost her Gift. And well before that, you didn't use your chance at Galdor to hurt her either. Not in the way she hurt you."

I instinctually held my shoulder where Molly bit down during our first combat exam. It had mended so well that only the outline remained. "That feels so long ago," I admitted.

"That's because it's not who either of you are now."

***

A month went by.

Every week, the Divine Observer documented the increasing downcast toll and reminded Gifteds that their Gift would be safe once Cassius was king. Every day, I awoke from his intrusion and stared up at the fractured ceiling—splintering, splintering apart. Pieces fell along my face overnight. And every chance, we kept our eye on Molly. She hugged the wall less.

We all made a point of eating together since the Determination.

Persephone and Kai argued over the answer to one of our exam questions when a spider's crawl stalked down my spine, its web entangling me to him.

The tables, the students, the condensation on water glasses—everything vanished away just as the cathedral did during Queen Maya's coronation. Just as Cassius showed me his perspective while holding Melanie hostage in Cherryville.

The four walls remained grey but thinned and narrowed into a hallway. Large murals covered these walls in a long row, each perfectly aligned with the other.

Where am I?

Here, I stopped—or rather Cassius stopped—in front of one of the paintings as if to give a response.

Two children held hands loosely by the fingers. Their connected, raised hands served as the focal point; tethered but out of photographic obligation rather than desire like forced friends or relatives. The girl stood on the left. Yellow hair curled and framed around her heart-shaped face. Light blue and white cloth ruffled and layered her body, and small star-shaped earrings brightened her face. Her posture stood between straightened and slouched, her lips and cheeks soft and distant like she was bored.

Oh, but those shark eyes I could recognize from anywhere. Black ink pierced through her gaze. This had to be Skylar as a child.

Which meant that the boy next to her...could that really be Cal? Completely muted of all emotion, he stood so rigid beside Skylar I thought he'd snap into two. A black blazer and bow tie decorated his form in professional attire, a blue lapel matching Skylar's dress. Even now, his face blurred with the grey background as if the painter became careless, less intentional with his features compared to hers.

A metal rod drilled through Cal's stomach in my mind's eye, splitting his body in half. The Norburn incident stormed my thoughts, reminding me of my failures to stop the Diviner.

Blood pooled from the painting as Cal's head warped in an egg-like shape. Black swirling the features of his face into a screech. Red ink covered their hands, so thick it appeared as though nothing existed past their wrists.

Still through his perspective, Cassius moved on, waving away a servant who nodded at him. Was he a guest at the Stanton mansion? How was that possible? No, the Stantons would know him on sight. He couldn't possibly be a guest. If he wasn't, then perhaps the AGM had overtaken the staff. But if he was—then he could have the Stanton family under his influence. I didn't know what to do with my uncertainty. Should I warn Skylar? Or imply to Queen Maya that his new hideout was in plain sight?

I blinked and the tables, the students, my classmates—all came back into focus.

Wait 48 hours before you take action. His voice delicately weaved itself into my mind.

48? 48! How could I possibly wait that long knowing where he was now?

My mouth twitched in my hesitation.

"Something you want to say Nora?" Leo prompted across the table. I side-glanced in his direction as everyone's focus turned toward me. The strain in my face tightened.

"*Skylar,*" my mouth drew her name out as if I was speaking it for the first time.

How's your family doing? I thought but couldn't dare say out loud.

She looked at me expectedly, those black eyes squinted and confused. Irritation began to etch into her expression.

I had to say something. Say something!

"Why don't you talk about Cal?"

Dread pooled into my heart as the question hung in the air. With one hand, Skylar could push the air and leave the question flying into orbit, but she pulled at her sleeves instead. Everyone shifted in their seat with her, alarm imprinted on their faces.

"Why the sudden interest?" Skylar asked, her teeth exposed from a hostile smile.

My hand clutched the inside of my forearm, but I halted before any anxious ticks gave way to exposure. I needed to create a convincing response, one that was genuine.

"There's no sudden interest," I assured, "I just haven't been brave enough to ask. You don't talk about him very often."

"Yeah? Why would I when he's dead?"

My shoulders tensed. "I guess you're right. I think about my lost love, but I don't like talking about her with others. She was another Unfortunate servant."

Molly twirled the fork in her hands and lowered her head.

"I don't need your sob story," Skylar retorted. "And I certainly don't need you trying to relate to me."

She pressed forward after a deep breath. "You want to hear me talk about Cal? Here you go. We were betrothed at ten, he had blond hair that got lighter in the summer, and I was cruel to him. Is there anything else you'd like to know?"

"You were betrothed at ten?" The question spilled out, both a confirmation of the painting and of a horrifying fact.

Skylar leaned back in her chair and crossed her arms defensively, her words quickening.

"Is there a problem with that? It's very normal in my House to secure the next generation. We need pure Auran blood, and Cal provided that lineage. There was no need for courtship or hesitation or other suitors. Why does it matter to you?"

"Just ten years old." I couldn't help but dig deeper into her anger. My voice lowered, "It's just that I was chosen for servitude at ten years old."

Skylar's mouth opened and stayed open for way longer than it should.

"Are you intentionally trying to piss me off?"

"No!" I waved my hand in front of myself, her glare too sharp for me to look back. "I was just thinking about your family. You know with how Molly..."

I trailed off as concern flushed Skylar's face at the mention of her House, realizing how close I slipped into dangerous territory.

Molly dropped her fork, the clatter erupting like thunder. How many minutes were in 48 hours? I couldn't keep this up for a mere five.

"Sorry, I won't—I won't ask again."

I retreated. Neither of us spoke for the rest of our meal.

Photographs on an Old Dresser

The next day, Skylar's name was removed from the daily assignments, and her presence was nonexistent at morning practice.

Panic seeped into my every pore. I hardly said anything to her since yesterday. We were barely at the 24-hour mark since

Cassius's demanded timeframe.

As Isaac discussed the first drills and completely ignored her absence, Leo and Persephone glanced at each other in silent acknowledgment. I slowly approached.

"What are you two planning?" I asked.

"If she is still on campus, we can most likely intercept her at the dorm or at the gate," Persephone noted.

Fern and Kai slowly approached too, Fern more obvious out of the two. Molly remained still, but even with her back turned, I knew she was listening. We all suddenly had a new mission: find Skylar and understand why she was missing.

"Kai, Leo, and I will take the gate if she's there," I ordered quickly. "Persy, Fern, and Molly can take the dorm."

"Hey!" Frost left Isaac Winter's breath. "Pay attention and separate."

Leo leaned in and whispered, "We'll signal, and you run."

"*Now!*" Isaac yelled.

We awkwardly dispersed at his command.

Waiting for a signal, I kept the Mati siblings in my peripheral.

The room grew hotter—so hot I couldn't see Isaac's breath anymore.

He noticed, eyes flickering to Leo and Persephone. The twins yelled out, and we used that as the signal to sprint.

Isaac retaliated quickly, swiping his hand across the air downward—close to our feet. But the ice turned to mist, cloaking us in shadow as we fractured off into two groups.

Draped in a long-sleeve white dress with blue ribbon similar to her painting, Skylar stood alongside Minister Gabriel at the front gate. The metal lurched back; we raced against its opening.

"Stanton!" She froze at Leo's calling and turned to us.

Hunched over, we caught our breaths.

"What are you doing?" she demanded.

"Why aren't you—why aren't you at practice?" Leo demanded back.

She scoffed and raised her nose, twirling the parasol in her hands. "So rude, all of you asking me these questions. I'm going to Caliel *if* you must know."

"What?" I was thankful we all asked at the same time. Their confusion laced well with my fear.

"Ugh, more questions!" Skylar shook her head, turning her attention to me. "*Your* stupid questions got me paranoid, thinking about Cal. So, I called my House. Servants responded but said neither of my parents were available until tomorrow. After what happened with Molly…"

She trailed off, but her face hardened into hopeful determination. "I need to go check for myself if my family is still there. My mother would tell me if they went out."

No, no no, no, no! It wasn't nearly enough time. Cassius had to be the reason why they were "unavailable" until tomorrow.

Anxiety lurched in my stomach. *Please*, I begged him, *please Cassius. Don't hurt her for my mistake.*

"If you're done, we can get on our way," prompted Minister Gabriel.

"Yes, and what are you doing here, Minister Gabriel?" I narrowed my eyes at him.

"Miss Stanton and I are going to Caliel together." I hated his pretentious voice, the way his words always spoke down to me. "It's where my ministry was founded, and it's where she needs me."

"Sneaking out wasn't working for any of us," Skylar clarified, "so I went over Isaac Winter's head. My family regularly attended Minister Gabriel's sermons when he was the regional head minister there."

"I trust you're not hoping to join us," added Minister Gabriel.

My jaw tightened.

Kai stepped in. "We insist, minister."

I hated how Minister Gabriel's brown eyes visibly lightened by the Mare's sight, how his lips curled in a half-sneer when talking.

"Then join you may, Mr. Lancer. But we may return late from traveling."

He turned to me. "I would hate for you to break the 8th law of servitude."

The one you created, I thought bitterly.

I would usually step closer as an intimidation tactic, but I didn't want to be any closer to such a retched man.

"Do not fret, minister," I replied. "Molly Montgomery is coming along, too. I won't be without my House."

He stared straight through me for more heartbeats than I cared for, but I wasn't going to look away first. I wasn't going to give him that satisfaction.

He grumbled, "Very well. Then you'll have no trouble carrying Miss Stanton's parasol for her during the journey."

"And why would I do that, minister?"

"Because an Unfortunate servant must carry out any and all orders given by their Gifted House and those their Gifted House permits. Surely, you haven't forgotten the first Unfortunate Law, and surely Miss Montgomery isn't in a position to deny the request."

I bit the inside of my lip, split between obedience and defiance. "Surely not," I matched his tone, reaching for Skylar's parasol but Skylar retracted, and Leo caught it at the same time. Persy shot her hand up in a jagged movement, worry flashing her features in case he accidentally sparked a flame.

He didn't. Instead, he and Skylar glanced at each other sheepishly before he released it to her.

She opened the parasol on her own and addressed Minister Gabriel, "I already planned on traveling alone. Nothing changes if they come along."

We parted for Caliel. I purposely sat closer to Molly than I usually would so that anytime Minister Gabriel even tried looking in my direction, he would see my protection.

Several hours went by with little conversation. My thoughts all-consuming, I didn't remember entering city limits or the city for that matter.

If Cassius was still inside the Stanton House, we were surely in danger. But if I somehow found him without the others, then maybe they'd have a chance even if I didn't. And if he wasn't still there, perhaps I could find evidence that he had and use that as a way to tell the others.

He didn't say anything as I thought of all the possibilities.

Arriving at the Stanton mansion, I moved close to Skylar's side.

"Where are 12 and 16 to greet me?" Skylar noticed the lack of servants at the front door and ran forward, carelessly pushing the doors open herself. I sprinted into action, Leo the fastest to keep up behind me.

Stepping into the foyer was like stepping into another world. So large, glorious, and lonely. The ceiling stretched upwards to the heavens, but there wasn't time for details.

Skylar lifted herself into the air and leaped over staircases, weaving in and out of corridors with ease. The others tried following, but I didn't turn around to find out.

The halls looked exactly as they did in my vision. We continued to follow her.

Passing the painting, I halted. It appeared exactly as it did when I first saw it—two children loosely connected to each other without distortion.

Skylar continued to dart through her house, determined to find a soul. We hadn't found one yet.

The wind carried each step, propelling her forward as she shouted out to the empty halls, but family portraits only glared down in silence.

She shouted more numbers, I realized, instead of names—all in sporadic order.

Rounding a corner further away from us, Skylar and another woman screamed. Something shattered on the wooden floor.

"Oh, 24!" Relief washed over Skylar's face.

We caught up, entering an informal dining room that connected to the kitchen. A servant stood, dumbfounded, holding an empty tray and looking down at a broken tea set. Leftover amounts of honey, cinnamon, and lemon also lined the floor.

Skylar continued, "I'm glad to see that the house isn't completely empty. Where are 12 and 16? They're supposed to be at the door. And 13, 4, and 29 aren't in their usual stations, either."

The servant just looked at me.

"Don't mind my guests," Skylar redirected her attention. "Answer my question this instant."

"Apologies, Miss Stanton," the servant continued to look dazed at the chaos around her. "I can't seem to concentrate today. We're recently understaffed, ma'am."

"Understaffed? Where is Mr. Stanton?" Skylar demanded.

"I need to speak with him right away."

"Of course, ma'am. He's in the Great Hall. I'll let you know you're here." The servant squeezed herself past me to enter the hallway and began walking over to two large doors at the far end. But Skylar picked up speed and threw open the doors with her Gift.

I only caught a glimpse of Mr. Stanton—a tall and thin navy blue pinstriped suit and whitening blond hair—before the doors closed by the wave of his hand and the servant blocked our path.

"Apologies, miss, but Mr. Stanton only meets with his family members and those who have an appointment."

I didn't see Cassius in my momentary glance, but he *was* here. I felt his presence, just like when we rescued Melanie.

"Are guests not permitted to join their host?" I asked.

"Apologies, miss," the servant repeated. "No they are not unless explicitly permitted by Mr. Stanton."

Minister Gabriel finally caught up with us, panting from the run. "I have an appointment!" he called.

The servant frowned. "Mr. Stanton does not have an appointment with anyone today, I'm afraid. Did you not receive the cancellation notice, sir?"

"*Cancellation* notice?" The minister used the rest of his lung capacity to cough. He marched forward, his face darkening into a red hue. "I received no cancellation notice!"

I stepped in between them as he shouted, "You open that door right now and—"

"None of us are getting into that room, minister," I cut him off. "Leave her alone."

He stopped, breathing hard with his mouth open. I pushed into the servant more to distance myself until he finally stepped back.

He grumbled something about Unfortunates before he straightened his posture and adjusted his tie.

"If Mr. Stanton will not see me today, may I chat with Mrs. Stanton instead?"

"Apologies, sir," the servant sheepishly responded. "Mrs. Stanton is ill today."

The tea, I thought. It was something I would offer Mrs. Montgomery if she were sick. Was that true or did Cassius get to her?

Minister Gabriel gritted his teeth. "A reschedule then?"

"Of course, minister. You can talk to 3 in the front office. I must remain here and attend to Mr. Stanton, so I am not permitted to walk you there. Please understand, sir."

"I understand that Mr. Stanton is a busy man," he grumbled. "Good day."

I didn't watch him walk away. I needed to find Cassius or any evidence that he was here. When I headed his instructions in Cherryville, Melanie's Gift was safe and he was gone. We entered the Stanton House before the 48-hour ban lifted, so why did everything appear almost normal? Missing Unfortunates, an unexpected meeting cancellation, and Mrs. Stanton's illness were all I could rely on.

I needed to explore.

Leo had the same idea. "We'll wait for our *lovely* friend to return," he said with a fake chirp. He crept behind Kai and grabbed his shoulders, pulling him along. "In the meantime, we'll explore this *lovely* home."

The servant hesitated. "Feel free, sir."

We all shifted in a wave, turning from the door. My stare lingered on the servant who only stared back, unblinking. The more fear she tried to hide from her features, the more I needed to find out if she was an AGM member in disguise.

We retreated back down the hall. I caught sight of the large mural of Skylar and Cal as children again, both unaware that he would die eight years later. If I did find Cassius here, I prayed for different results.

Persephone approached her brother staring up at the painting, too. "What is the plan?" she asked.

I framed my words carefully. "If Skylar is concerned, then we should fan out and try to find anything related to the Diviner or AGM here."

"I can take Molly and Fern—you take Kai and Leo?"

No, I thought. I needed to look alone.

"How about we separate on our own?" I asked. I could hear how stupid it sounded coming from my mouth, and Persy caught on.

"It would be much safer to go in at least pairs."

I bit the inside of my lip. "Right."

We split off at the top of the first staircase: Leo led me and Kai to the left and Persephone led Molly and Fern to the right.

Leo's eyes scanned about. I did the same. What was *he* looking for?

Though grand, the layout of the house was surprisingly straightforward. Tall walls adorned with Stanton legacy repeated with every grand staircase. Golden labels resided next to closed doors; I tried reading each one—looking for anything that might suggest Cassius's presence.

Where are you? I demanded.

He didn't respond.

Unfortunates rarely treaded our path. Each servant kept their heads down and mouths tightly shut. I stared as we passed; they brushed closer to the walls.

"Here we go." Leo broke the silence and stopped in front of a room with two doors that pushed inward. The label read: Cal

Hilfrey.

My eyes widened. "What are we doing here, Leo?"

"I'm doing a small pickup," he replied.

"A small *what?*" Kai spoke in disbelief.

Leo grabbed the handle and shook. Locked.

"Damn," Leo sighed. "I could have used Persy. Oh well."

With the snap of his fingers, a flame ignited.

Kai pushed him back from the door, and the fire in Leo's hand dimmed. "You're not *seriously* considering breaking into a dead man's room, are you?"

Leo professed a disappointed sound. "And here I thought you were going to help me." He pointed at me. "Nora, you're up. Sword time."

I stood straighter as the two looked expectantly at me. "What's so important in there, Leo?" I asked.

"That is between me and my client."

Kai huffed. "You can be so arrogant sometimes, Leo. Skylar will only hate you more if you go in there."

"It's a calculated risk."

"Don't try and win me over with that. I'm doing the calculations, and they don't add—"

Leo sparked a raging flame that melted off the exposed lock.

"—up!" Kai and I jumped back. Heat flushed my face.

Molten dripped between the two door frames; Leo kicked them in.

No going back now. I stepped in as Kai stared, jaw-slacked.

"Hey Kai," Leo called, "would you mind being the lookout? Wouldn't want us to get caught."

"Wouldn't want *us* to get caught," Kai mimicked Leo in an agitated high-pitched remark as he turned to the hallway.

Cal's room appeared bare with little personality. He had a

drawer and a desk and a bed. He had a closet—once closed that Leo opened—filled with blue patterned clothes, varying from athletic to business.

He had a dresser and a mirror resting on top with pictures taped along the frame. A gradual change showcased here: as a child and tween, Skylar stared with a blank-faced expression and often alongside Cal—like a servant captured the moment between them at church or at a party or in training.

More depicted her as a teen and especially as a young adult. In one faded photo, she sat at a table drinking coffee, and in another, she stood on top of a mountain, triumphant and glistening in sweat.

Her lips slowly, slowly gleamed at the person behind the lens. From his lack of appearance, she smiled from Cal's point of view. She smiled at Cal.

Leo used his scared arm to gently pluck the photo of Skylar standing on a rock facing the wilderness, her arms and legs outstretched wide in a victorious pose, and her expression joyful. He carefully pocketed it to make sure the edges didn't bend.

"Is that for your client, too?" I asked sarcastically.

"It will be." He began thumbing through Cal's dresser and then his desk. Clearly, he wasn't budging.

I glanced around myself, though I doubted they would stick any guest in here. Even if he was here without the Stanton's knowledge, hiding in the closed-off room of a man he killed would be too cruel and on-the-nose, even for someone like Cassius. No sign of him or the AGM. I didn't know whether to sigh in disappointment or relief.

Leo stashed some papers in the other pocket. "All right, let's go," he said quickly. He spoke louder, "Kai, are we clear?"

"No!" Kai snarked back. He gestured to the two door

frames broken wide open. "You can't hide this! They'll know it was us!"

Leo stepped back into the hallway with a casually dismissive tone. "We'll be out of here before they can do anything. Besides, we're guests. Guests of wealthy people can get away with plenty."

We started walking back from where we came; Kai caught up with us. "Guests are supposed to be cordial, but it's your funeral."

Persephone came into view first from the opposite side, followed by Fern and Molly—both with wary expressions.

We caught up with the others at the center at the base of the fourth-floor staircase. The Mati siblings started firing off their observations.

"What did you find on the right side?" asked Leo.

"Straightforward hallways and rooms," Persephone started, "Empty guest accommodations each with their own bathroom, four broom closets, a large kitchen, and a formal and the informal dining room. We also found something, but we can discuss that later. What did you find on the left side?"

"Same straightforward hallways. Three parlors, all the House rooms, four broom closets, seven office spaces, and more rooms of little interest. Did you check the second floor?"

"Yes. The formal dining room is right above the Grand Hall, but it's wooden floors so we heard ourselves a lot more than we heard below us. I imagine when it's a party, you can hear every conversation happening above you in that office."

"So that's an out. Any vents?"

"None that are large enough for us to crawl in."

"Hm. If there's nothing behind that, the hallway is the only way in and out of that room. We'd have to press our ears to the door."

"Can't do that with the servant there."

"No," Leo agreed. "Did you check the rooms to the left and right? How are they walled?"

"The right is a bust but the room on the left is longer. That wall runs along the side of the Grand Hall. It's not ideal but we could press our ears to it there."

"Do you think the servant would mind?"

"If she gives us any trouble, I think we can handle ourselves."

The twins blinked at each other, finally pausing.

Leo smiled, "We still got it."

Persephone shook her head. "You had your fun. Come along."

"What, follow your mischief more?" Kai scoffed.

"Yep," Leo grabbed his hand, and that was that.

We crammed together in the room directly to the left of the Grand Hall, our faces squished against the wall that separated the two spaces. The Mati siblings shushed us as we adjusted to our new places.

Skylar and her father's voices traveled just as well as they did underwater. I frowned.

But after a minute of their sounds rising like bubbles, the door burst open from Skylar's Gift. We saw her stumble out from the crack in the door; the servant stepped all the way back and out of view.

"I must be going," her polite tone faltered.

Mr. Stanton strode out on his own Gift. "We don't have a choice!" A despondent confidence laced his words. "Think about your mother."

"Think about yourself!" Skylar whipped around to face him. "That's all you're doing."

She turned back to leave, but her father caught up and

grabbed ahold of her arm.

"Where is this coming from?" The sincerity in his question became lost in his decisive statement, "What I do is for *your* future. *Our* legacy, Skylar."

He looked down and pulled her sleeve up to expose her scars. "What are these?"

She pulled away, a deep and frustrated sigh escaping her lips. She looked down and crossed her arms like a girl does when she's in trouble.

"They're nothing."

"They make you look like a Mati."

"Let me think on it, Dad," she changed the conversation.

He opened his mouth to disagree but sighed too. "I pray that you are given more time."

They stood in silence for several heartbeats.

"I must be going," Skylar said again. She turned to the servant and asked, "Where are my classmates?"

24 swallowed hard. "They're exploring, ma'am."

"Exploring?!" Mr. Stanton boomed.

Skylar placed her hand out to him and he stopped. "I know where at least one went. If Nora has any hand at play, they're all together, too. Thank you, 24."

The servant blinked and her eyebrows slightly raised, the only indication of her surprise. I remembered when Mr. Harris gave me a "thank you." Its rarity was always noted.

"Right, well, safe journeys back, Skylar." Mr. Stanton tipped his hat. "Make your decision soon."

He withdrew back into the Grand Hall.

Skylar inhaled cautiously, put on a hardened expression, and started walking down the hallway.

Persephone pushed us out with haste, but there wasn't a way for us to backtrack and appear in front of her. We all stumbled into the hallway after her. The servant gave us an alarmed look; Skylar heard the commotion and turned toward us with a suspicious expression.

"What's all this?" She crossed her arms.

"Just done exploring," said Leo.

Her eyes rolled. "What did you hear?"

"Nothing."

"I'm not in the mood." Skylar glanced at each of us. "Who is going to give me a straight answer?"

Molly piped up, "It was just the tail end, but..." The words jumbled in her throat. "Skylar, has your mother been downcasted?"

"What?" I stepped out and looked back and forth between the two girls.

Molly continued, "We found her on accident. She looks, well she looks like how I did, Skylar."

"It's none of your business," Skylar said quickly, turning and storming down the hallway.

We followed her pace.

"But that means Cassius was here!" I pushed.

I peered to the servant still within earshot at the end of the hallway. She kept still and silent, pressing herself further into the wall.

Pieces clicked into place. The AGM newspaper printed the increasing number of downcasted souls for four weeks straight. Stirred fear into the hearts of Gifteds. Steered them toward the Diviner. One of my initial suspicions were right, but I didn't want to be right.

"*Skylar,*" I said in a sharp whisper.

"What?" She whipped around. We were so close to the exit.

"Did your father pledge his allegiance to the Diviner?"

Skylar looked down, her jaw tightening and her shoulders

tensing. Her silence pierced us.

"It's none of your business," she whispered.

"None of our—" I started.

"That's right!" The wind picked up around the Aura. "My father..." She faulted, failing to find words that would save him from scrutiny.

"Is committing treason against the crown," I finished for her.

"Keep your voice down!"

"Do you really expect me to be silent about this?" I stepped forward. "For any of us?"

"Could you?" she begged. "I haven't decided what to do yet myself." Her words lowered; she turned away to wipe her eyes and opened the doors with her Gift. She started walking to the waiting car but halted again.

I walked after her, but several hands slowed me down. I looked at Fern and Molly. "You're not seriously considering—"

I looked at the rest of my classmates. They all looked back at me with cautious faces.

"*All* of you are considering?" I couldn't even finish my question.

"I don't like it," Kai admitted, "but..."

"She hasn't chosen to go along with it yet," Fern finished.

"She hasn't chosen if she's staying, either," I countered.

You haven't chosen either, Cassius reminded.

My mouth went dry.

Confliction festered within my heart. I was hiding my psychic connection with Cassius from all of them for my own protection. All so they wouldn't label me a traitor and turn me in to Minister Gabriel. I hated the system he perpetuated, but I also hated how the AGM handled their freedom. At the same time, I couldn't figure out another option, nor could I deny how effective the AGM were. I promised Valerie to escape servitude at any chance, and I fulfilled that promise by becoming Iridion's first Unfortunate soldier. But that spiraled into something greater and far more complex than I initially realized, and it wasn't enough for the rest of us. I wanted better for the rest of us.

I had no right to ask Skylar to decide now between her family and her country, but I wanted her to decide. I hoped then it would be easier for me to do the same.

I continued looking at the rest of my friends. Leo, Persephone, and Molly—they all shared a similar view with the others.

Maybe I was wrong. Maybe they wouldn't label me a traitor if I told them after all.

I caved, "Fine. I'll…I'll keep to secrecy as long as you do."

I could trust my friends. I needed to trust my friends.

My heart struck rapidly, spreading a sickly fire within my chest. *I have my own confession,* I repeated the words in my mind, hoping they would come out of my swelling throat. *I have my own confession.*

"I—"

"May I ask you to continue your conversation in the car or on the train home?" Minister Gabriel appeared at the bottom of the stairs, the car door now opened. "It's dreadfully impolite to keep company waiting."

I bit down on my tongue hard to keep my appearance from completely giving myself away. My heartbeat still rapidly pressed against my chest; the burn did not subside.

"Our apologies, minister." Skylar gave her best performance, too, her voice light and sincere. "We are coming now. I'm sorry you couldn't see my father today."

We shuffled to the car with her, an aura of concealment thick in the air.

Scrunched together in a small space, the silence was deafening. No one dared ask me what I was trying to say lest our secrecy come to light. Thankfully Minister Gabriel didn't ask me what I was trying to say before he cut me off because he didn't care for my voice.

We departed Caliel and headed back to Galdor Academy together.

Cassius whispered, his voice certain. *That was close. You won't do that again.*

CHAPTER SIXTEEN

What-Ifs

———

The crack in the ceiling became a fracture and now hovered over Fern on my left and was making its way across the room to Leo and Kai. Water dripped through the opening, splashing against my pillow and my face like rain. I had enough.

Ripping myself away from my dampening covers and nightmares, I reached upward. My arms were too short. I jumped onto the table beside my bed, its foundation wobbling from the sudden shift in weight.

"Nora?" I didn't know who said my name. Your voice registered in my mind.

Promise me.

My fingers caught a loose and wet piece; I peeled it away. My nails dug into the rough texture, clawing away at the remnants. I was sick of seeing this every morning. I was driven mad by what I couldn't stop. Cassius used both to taunt me. But this—this I had control over.

"Nora!"

I always thought about the what-ifs: what if I walked over after ten minutes of waiting? Six minutes? What if I walked over one second later or one second before? What if we didn't meet at the center of our dwellings at all—what if we met at my doorsteps or at the train station or in the bazaar? What if we left right then and there when we sealed our promise in Cherryville? What if I leaned in and kissed you after mending your wounds? Would we even be apart the following day? What if we left the Sunday train to Thunder Bay but redirected and landed in Stone Creek or Faywater or even as far as the sea on the other side of the continent? What if we got lost in the woods of Northbrook and decided to stay there, shaded and sheltered by the tall trees? What if Molly attacked you a week before it actually happened?

What if we didn't leave at all?

He made me relive it. I dreamed each scenario and played out each what-if as though I could go back and change anything at all. And this damned ceiling. The very walls would soon crumble around me.

You didn't hesitate to step into my place to accept my punishment as your own. Molly sank her teeth in deep; your body couldn't stop shaking. But despite your panting and screaming and bleeding, you still smiled at me when I finally decided to escape with you.

You still waited for me to say yes. You never abandoned me. You were perfect for the Anti-Gifteds Movement.

"Nora, stop!"

Someone picked me up, but I didn't know who. I thrashed, my eyes staring up, up, up.

When Mr. Harris invited me to Galdor Academy, I saw his relaxed posture and casual words and it ignited me to my core. I wanted to reach that feeling—of complete certainty and autonomy. That was my chance, and I still felt neither.

Did our promise even have meaning anymore?

"...Nora?"

My neck snapped upward; the Senior circle stared at me expectantly. How long had I been here? I thumbed over the bandages on my fingers. When did Kai do this?

"What, ma'am?" I asked.

Queen Maya repeated herself, "What are your thoughts?"

"Oh," my voice was low. I scrambled to respond quickly, "yeah, that sounds good."

Queen Maya squinted. "You approve of Minister Gabriel's proposal?"

"I *what*?" My eyes widened at the mistake. "I—no. No. I don't—forgive me. What did Minister Gabriel propose?"

Minister Gabriel feigned irritation, but a hidden smirk revealed his pleasure in my obliviousness.

"The AGM situation is worsening. As we continue to search for their camps, I think it will be important to strengthen our curfew law: include all Unfortunates instead of just servants and start the curfew earlier in the evening."

I could kill him right now. He was merely across the table; I could reach him and slice his chest open. I could watch his guts splatter to the floor before Isaac froze me in place. I could prove him right all along about me.

My gaze went to Mercy who was standing along the wall behind him. She entertained the baby Prince Henry. With so many Royal Crest Knights working around the clock, Queen Maya kept her younger brother close the way she couldn't with the older. I addressed Minister Gabriel instead of killing him. My words were slow and level-headed, a slow-boiled anger that resembled Gifted business politeness.

"Minister, you have managed to add two more

Unfortunate Laws to our already oppressed lives. It's a marvelous feat all in itself, and the AGM mark your victory by aiding their cause. Are you so dense that you can't see it? Or do you just refuse to?"

Queen Maya gave me a warning look, but I continued. What could a Lux do against me?

"The Divine Observer is scaring Gifteds—your so-called people. So could you *please* take the AGM seriously before you bring an unraveling to this kingdom? You are constantly falling right into the Diviner's hands."

Before more Gifteds turned allegiance. I wanted to tell them about Mr. Stanton, but I didn't. I needed to keep my promises.

"You claim that *I* am the one aiding this kingdom to ruin?" Minister Gabriel latched onto my final words. "Your presence here is far worse than mine, or have you forgotten how the AGM used your insolence in the press before? Gifteds already astray like Mr. Harris only serve to confuse your place. Not to mention your disgusting influence on Prince Cassius! The way he looked at you pushed him further away from the Divine's grace."

Dark red diminished all proper demeanor in my face, "He treated me with respect!"

"Downcasted souls don't deserve respect!" Minister Gabriel fired back. "You require retribution, sanction, salvation. You should be beneath him, not beside him!"

Glass shattered like lightning.

We flinched and turned to Mercy's direction. She quickly bent down and picked up as many shards as she could carry.

Prince Henry cried out in a high-pitched shriek.

Queen Maya and I rushed over.

"What happened?" she demanded.

"I'm so sorry, ma'am," Mercy said quickly. "I don't know

what happened. I—I wasn't holding the glass. It was on the table, and-and it wasn't even near the edge. I—I don't know how it fell."

It's happening so soon? Cassius's voice floated around me. *Not even a year old and already learning. Fascinating.*

Awestruck, my voice registered at a whisper, "It's his Animus Gift."

He wiggled in the cradle, his features scrunched at the center in discontent. As he wailed, I picked him up on instinct as Mercy placed the broken glass on the table nearby.

"Careful!" Queen Maya reached out and quickly retreated. "Gifts are at their strongest and most unpredictable as children."

I pretended that Prince Henry was nothing more than a mere baby. Rotating slowly, I nestled him close to my chest and sang in a low hum. He pushed against me, but I insisted until he relaxed and his doughy blue eyes struggled to stay awake.

"There," I placed him gently in his crib.

Queen Maya rubbed her thumbs together, her hands resting near her neck. Mercy noticed. "What's troubling you, ma'am? Is there anything I can get you?"

"From now on, Prince Henry stays alongside me as you do," the queen commanded.

Her Unfortunate servant nodded. "Yes, ma'am." We noticed how the queen picked at her gloves. "Anything else, ma'am?"

"We still need to show the government is sovereign and stronger than the Diviner. That way, Gifteds don't panic and feed the AGM more," Queen Maya expressed.

"You want to put up a façade?" Isaac Winters joined the conversation.

Queen Maya opened her mouth, but she groaned instead, pressing her hand against her forehead and gritting her teeth. I looked at Prince Henry; he stirred but didn't cry out.

"Ma'am?" Mercy asked.

"Queen Maya?" I cautiously stepped forward. "What's wrong?"

"Nothing," she murmured. Still rubbing her forehead, the queen threw her voice out there as if she wasn't quite sure and answered Isaac's question. "No, I need to find a new way to reach my subjects. How can we reassure their trust in us?"

I knew my answer immediately, *We don't.*

Queen Maya grunted again, tilting and holding herself steady on the table. With her Nox Gift pushing us away, we could only watch.

But the headache faded as quickly as it came. Her blue eyes lit up, and she looked off as though figuring out her thoughts.

"Have we considered a royal ball?" she asked.

Silence enveloped the room. Where did that idea come from?

"Do you think that's wise?" I questioned.

"Use the proper terms when addressing your queen," the minister snapped.

My jaw tightened. "Do you think that's wise, ma'am?"

Queen Maya patted an index finger on her cheeks in thought. "If it's confined, I think so." She pondered the possibility over, a smile slowly forming on her face as a royal ball become more and more plausible.

"A wonderful idea, Your Majesty," Mercy encouraged.

What? I thought in disbelief.

"It would be a great way to showcase your status as sovereign," Minister Gabriel agreed.

I turned to him. Whether he actually liked the idea or not,

I couldn't decipher.

Unbelievable. I could think of one person who loved large public events with the most elite people there.

Despondency rooted itself in my heart. My voice didn't matter, did it?

The minister said something about the coronation and its security. That this would be another demonstration of power and wealth reachable through a camera lens. Queen Maya latched on harder and harder.

Another pointless waste of time. But I didn't say that. I pleaded for Minister Gabriel to take the AGM seriously. I should have pleaded with Queen Maya, too.

Isaac concentrated on the security measures for the event. I watched them chat as I retreated back into my what-ifs once more.

What if I died and you were invited to Galdor Academy instead? Would you have done anything differently? Would you let Gifteds destroy themselves as they so clearly wanted to do?

Queen Maya twisted around and finally acknowledged me but the decision was already made.

She offered her gloved hand to me, "Would you like to learn how to dance, Nora?"

INTERLUDE 4

Rain fell amid the grey haze, soaking through my clothes. A pale pink dress. Huddled, crammed together. With other dresses. Other Unfortunate women my age.

I searched for your face, but every detail blurred around me. I knew none of them, and I knew all of them.

We waited to be chosen.

A familiar Gifted stepped forward from the fog and outreached his hand in my direction. The other girls washed away with the growing darkness; the rain loudened to static background noise. Everything else was behind me.

Would you dance with me, Nora? he whispered.

I inhaled to start my rehearsed answer, but my words caught in my throat. We had stood frozen like this for so long.

Why was I always ignoring what was in front of me? Nothing was going to change if I didn't take the first step forward. I did it once when I chose to keep your promise. I could...I could be brave again. And Queen Maya was handing him his perfect second chance to seize the crown.

Yes, that was it. If I accepted his offer, I could learn his next move. That was why...that *had* to be why I reached back.

"Yes."

My fingers folded with his with ease.

The dark blue coloring of the world shifted to a warm yellow glow, and Cassius stood in a sharp charcoal grey suit and dress shoes. Wrapping his other hand around my waist, he pulled me closer. My body molded with his with ease.

Marble walls and gold lining formed around us and became a ballroom. Trained Unfortunate servants moved their arms in rhythmic movements along one wall, filling the large space with pleasant string music. Gifteds in dazzling dresses floated along the polished floor.

He led me into his dance.

My steps mirrored with his with ease. His heartbeat reverberated in my soul. I squinted at that smile. *Focus.*

"What are you planning, Cassius?"

"You are so bright tonight. Stunning."

Wh— I followed his gaze and looked down at myself. A pale purple heart-shaped bust caught my eye first. The dress cinched my waistline before falling away into a long skirt, the fabric light and swaying with our movements. Sleeves rested lower on my shoulder, covering my forearm in more thin material and exposing my collarbone. A short silver pendant rested around my neck.

I looked back up. "Is this how I look to you? My color?"

"No."

He leaned closer; I forced my face to remain still. His blue eyes enveloped my sight; his starry night became my world. I couldn't possibly count every emotion dotted along his iris.

"You're not quite a color. You're..." He trailed off, trying to find the right words. "You're the absence of darkness. The void I see in other Unfortunates…I don't see in you."

He pulled away; I forced my face to remain still. Extending his hand out and guiding my back, Cassius spun me in sync with the faceless Gifteds around us. He brought me back to his chest.

I shakily exhaled, both determined and distracted. "What

are you planning, Cassius?"

"I'm planning..." He trailed off in a soft voice I thought I lost. "nothing. I already have exactly what I want right here."

My heart sank. I hated how his cheeky smile deepened as he recognized my thoughts. I tried again.

"You know your sister is exposing herself with this royal ball idea. What are you going to do with that information?"

"Are you enjoying our dance, Nora? I imagine it drives Maya mad—" My breath hitched as he dropped me into a dip. He caught me, his hands pressed along the curve of my back and his face above mine. "—that she can't hold you the way I can."

We stared at each other. What did his sister's Gift have to do with our current situation?

He lifted me back up, his smile split between devious and genuine. "You should know my intentions, Nora."

Something heavy formed and rested on my head. Jewels roughly grazed my fingers, the curved points in a shape of something I refused to say lest he read my mind.

Cassius smiled. "All you need to know for now is I'm planning for our reunion, so you may stand beside me—when you choose to."

My eyes widened and my lips wired shut. Before I could muster a word. Before I could spiral—

"Cas!" A high-pitched shrill echoed through the ballroom.

He released me as we turned upwards.

Her face was considerably younger, and her smile was something I missed dearly.

Princess Maya peered down at her brother from the top of the staircase leading up to the throne. She gasped at the sight of him, clutching her mouth with gloved hands. Could this be one of her memories?

Cassius's lips remained smiling at the person he hated most.

Or was he showing me one of *his* memories?

She squealed and ran towards her older brother. He offered his open palm.

CHAPTER SEVENTEEN

Thunder & Lightning

Running into the recital hall the next day, I ignored the similarities between reality and dreams.

"You're here!" Fern released her hold on Kai.

"I'm not dancing." I marched toward Kai and tugged on his sleeve. "I need you to help me."

His eyebrow ruffled.

I explained further, "I need to do some research. Now. On Animus."

"You look stressed." Fern spun around my frame, her hand reaching for my branded one. "How about we dance our worries away?"

"I'm not dancing." I waved her hand away and kept my attention on Kai. "Please. I need someone who can help me read the text."

Kai glanced to Fern as though for help, but she shrugged and began spinning mindlessly away from us. "Don't look at me. I'm here to dance and de-stress."

My patience thinned as Kai struggled to respond fast enough. "I'm going to listen to our queen," he whispered.

Persephone stepped forward in my peripheral, and I noticed her brother's absence. "I'll go with you," she offered.

My go-to was Kai because he never passed a chance to be smart. But he was passing that chance, and I didn't have time to be picky. I needed whoever was willing.

"Let's go," I motioned to the door.

But Queen Maya came over as if appearing from thin air. Wasn't she supposed to be running a kingdom?

"You're here!" She clapped her gloves together.

"She's trying to leave, Your Majesty," Kai interjected.

"What?" Queen Maya's face fell. "I already excused two of your teammates from attending. Stay and learn how to dance."

"I-I can't, Your Majesty," I stammered. "I need to do research. I need to know everything about the Animus Gift since I can't see Mr. Harris."

I could better understand what Cassius would do with his power. I could stop him if I couldn't stop Queen Maya from her own ridiculousness.

"Nonsense." She offered me an eager grin. "I want my personal guard well acquainted with dancing. All the best diplomacy is done in ballrooms instead of meeting rooms. Besides, you'll be the first Unfortunate to dance publicly with a Gifted. Isn't that exciting?"

"No, ma'am, it's not exciting," my thoughts spilled out in rapid secession. "I can't dance, ma'am. Who will protect you while I'm dancing? I certainly cannot dance with *you*."

Red burned my face as my mouth came to an abrupt close; her stunned stare sliced right through me.

Queen Maya folded her hands together. Her shock retreated back into a stillness, a silent rage that matched against mine.

"Kneel."

My mouth hung open. "What?"

"Kneel and apologize, Nora. And you must address me with the proper title as 'Your Majesty' while we are not in private correspondence."

Anger continued to fester within my Unfortunate soul.

My fingers flexed erratically as the only release for my anger. "Did I hear you correctly, Your Majesty?"

"You did. I will not be treated this way anymore by you or anyone else in my court. Kneel and apologize, or I shall have you suspended."

The shortness of her words, the stern and detached tone of her voice...the smiling and cheerfully crying Princess Maya in my dreams was completely removed from herself as queen. If that was a memory, it surely stayed in the past. Hatred spiraled and burned my chest.

I hesitated for several heartbeats. I couldn't be suspended, but I only kneeled to one other person before and gave my loyalty. He was more deserving at the time.

My knee slowly reached the marble floor. Neck bent downward, I presented my sword. "Forgive me, Your Majesty. I spoke out of turn."

Lying straight through my teeth—I was getting better at that.

"You are forgiven."

Returning to my feet slowly, my head stayed down as if in a bow. I refused to look her in the eye.

Several seconds felt like minutes.

I broke the silence first, "Permission to be excused, Your Majesty."

Queen Maya's arms tensed as she thought the request over.

"Granted."

"Permission to go with her, Your Majesty," said Persephone.

A stiffened sigh. "Granted."

***

Persephone forced me to sit down by myself at a table, perhaps so I wouldn't explode on her either. But I couldn't help it. I needed to learn more about Animus now. Now! The overhead clock inside the library clicked faster and faster.

Why don't you talk to me? Cassius asked.

Not a chance, I thought back.

But I can tell you anything you'd like to know about my power.

You can tell me anything you'd like to.

"Here we are!" A single textbook thudded on the desk. Persephone opened the book where her thumb was thoughtfully placed.

"An Animus refers to the mind. This includes the ability to manipulate objects, read the thoughts of others, and even influence human actions. Gifted by the Divine to rule over His creation, the Animus Gift is only granted within the royal bloodline. King Alston was the first Animus in Iridion's existence and became Iridion's first king."

She looked up, and we blinked at each other.

"That's it?" I blurted. I already heard this in history class.

Persephone lightly shrugged her shoulders. "There's not much documented about the Gift itself. I imagine it's because it's so rare and something the royal family would want to keep secret. The less you know about a Gift, the more elusive and powerful it becomes."

My head fell into my hands; I sank further into despair.

Placing her forearms on the table, Persephone leaned forward. "What's on your mind, Nora?"

"If you're trying to be funny with a play on words, it's not funny."

"Worth a try."

I tapped my fingernails on the table, my lips tightly pressed together. "I appreciate you helping, Persy."

"It's no problem. What is it though, if I may ask?"

I wanted to tell her. I wanted to tell everyone. But after failing a few days prior, Cassius's words still weaved through my mind. The word 'won't' and his certainty scared me. Even though Persephone didn't have a family name to lose, she did have Leo. And Fern and Kai both had their own families to lose if Cassius saw to it. I wasn't going to put anyone else at risk of the Diviner's mercy. I still had no idea what he was fully capable of, and what I did know was horrifying.

"I just need to find Mr. Harris," I finally said. "He's the only key to understanding what an Animus can really do and what that means in the Diviner's hands. He'll know how to sort things out."

"Isn't he unavailable because his hand was cut off and he was downcasted? It's reasonable why he'd want to be left alone during that recovery process."

"Screw that!" I slammed my palms onto the table; the textbook jumped. "We need him."

Persephone waited before asking another question. "Have you tried his office for clues?"

His office? "I hadn't even considered—let's go right now!" I leaped over the table to reach Persephone. "Let's go!"

Hope sprouted in my soul and lightened my steps.

The path was easy to remember from the last time we snuck

in. I watched Persephone pick the lock; my impatience bubbled up as rapidly as my newfound mission.

Bursting through the door, I started rummaging through his papers in the leftmost cabinet.

I ignored how I followed a similar pattern to when Cassius and I looked for Mr. Harris's ID. I tried to ignore how the prince's body felt pressed against mine so he could turn me invisible to Mr. Harris's sudden return.

Opening the front drawer at his desk, a little black book greeted me. Perfect.

My eyes scanned through the book, too restless to actually understand any of the information.

"Persy," I prompted.

She leaned in from her careful watch outside.

"Do you think we could go to your secret hideout where we can read this? You know, the one with all the snacks? I need a place that's," I glanced around the office, "away from here."

I didn't want to be reminded of Cassius's breath against my cheek.

The hideout wasn't too far away, and the bolts were already loosened.

Crawling in, faint voices reverberated toward our direction.

We were not alone.

Persephone and I froze, listening in.

"I can't believe you insist on coming here," Skylar said.

"I did no such thing, princess," replied Leo. "This is the best place in Galdor, and you're the one who's paranoid about someone important finding you."

"Can you shut up?" Skylar snapped. She huffed and I could imagine how her nose raised. "You know what—you're absolutely right, Leo. I cannot be seen with someone with so little in their name."

"Just three little letters."

"Could you be offended at least once?"

"I'm always offended. You're just not used to someone talking back, princess."

"Refrain from the princess speak!"

Leo started gagging as air clenched in his throat. I moved forward on instinct to help, but Persephone lightly held my shoulder to stop me.

Skylar came into view along the edges of my sight, but Leo was still obscured.

She sighed irritably and released her hold. Wrappers wrinkled as she shoved snacks away. "Could you just stop at least once? I am an heiress if you're going to be snide."

A bag of chips popped open. "Fine," said Leo. "As long as you know next time you choke me, you better take me out to dinner first."

"Really?" Skylar scrunched her face in disgust.

I imagined Leo shrugged. "Those are the rules, *heiress*."

"Don't eat right now! And with your mouth open no less. So rude!"

"You want one?"

"No!"

"I have the cheese ones."

A hesitant silence. "What about the barbeque ones?"

"Right here."

Skylar caught a bag sailing in front of her.

Fire ignited as Leo brought a flame to his hand; the glow warmed Skylar's face and darkened her surroundings. "Now what are those to you, anyway?"

Skylar glanced down to her knee and hesitated. "Letters."

"You don't say."

"Letters *Cal* wrote me," Skylar clarified bitterly. "When he was...you know...here."

Leo leaned forward; a pile of papers came into view. "May I see?"

So Skylar was his "client." I wondered if she would approval of his retrieval methods.

"I'm sure you already had a good look when you retrieved them."

"Did not! I am a professional."

"*Fine.*" Paper crinkled as they exchanged hands. "Don't mess them up with your grubby cheese hands!"

"Don't mess them up with your BBQ ones."

Skylar sighed again. She paused as he flipped through them. "Thank you for getting them for me. I just keep looking at them and I just—I thought—it's going to be so ridiculous—do not make fun of me!"

"I won't! I won't," Leo assured.

"Okay." Skylar hesitated for a solid minute. "I just thought that I could finally...cry for a person."

"What do you mean?"

"I just mean Nora's stupid comment got to me about why I don't talk about Cal."

My head dived back to safety at the sound of my name. Crunch sounds emanated from the both of them, indicating that she didn't notice.

Slowly, I peeked again.

"It's because I didn't *know* him. No one knew him. And I thought that these letters would help me see him as a person, but they don't. It only reminds me of how he was forced to write them when we were engaged. I made fun of him and all the fake emotions he used."

Leo thought over what she confessed. "You cried

when...that thing happened."

"I cried for my family legacy—not for my dad or even my mom. The Stanton name is supposed to mean something the same way that you having no name means something."

"Ouch."

"Oh, please don't take it that way right now. I'm being serious I just—"

"Why are you coming to me for this then?" Leo interrupted.

"Because—" Skylar spoke out quickly and then went silent as she looked at him and then away. "You're the only one who is brutally honest with me. All the time. It's super annoying, but it means that I know I can get an honest answer from you. And..."

"And?"

"Oh, Divine, don't make me say it," Skylar rolled her eyes and kept her gaze away from him.

"Aaaaaaaand?"

"*And*," Skylar dragged out the word with less enthusiasm. Her voice got quieter and quieter as she spoke, "You *know*. The only reason we survived Ebony Nique was by working together, so you've...helped me before. I've never been able to direct lightning like that. Ever."

Silence.

"Stop smiling at me like that!" Skylar shouted. A cascade of wrappers crackled as she shoved him down, but he chuckled.

Leo's laughter grew and reverberated through the metal beneath our palms. Skylar sucked her teeth and sighed again. "You can stop laughing now."

"Fine, fine." He shifted back to serious, laying the papers down somewhere in his snack pile. "Do they hurt at all? Your hands?"

Skylar pulled on her sleeve to hide them, but Leo's back caught my sight as he closed the space and used his burned hand to cup hers. Her breath hitched at the sudden action; the flame in his other hand dimmed, concentrating like his eyes along her markings.

"They don't hurt." Her voice was alarmed and muted, acutely aware of his closeness to her.

Leo continued to move her wrist gently.

Skylar inhaled sharply and pulled away. "Okay, that's enough." Darkness snuffed out for a heartbeat before Leo reignited it in his palm; they stared at each other.

"They don't hurt," she repeated in a low, unsteady voice I didn't recognize as hers.

"Sorry." Leo retracted until I couldn't see him again. Skylar sat back up in a sitting position. "They just remind me of lightning, actually. In a good way."

Skylar played with her wrists as they fell back into silence. We needed to leave. But just as I was about to signal to Persephone my suggestion, Leo's voice reflected caution.

"Skylar?"

"Hm?"

"Do you know what you're going to do about your father?"

Stillness thickened the air. "I don't know, Leo."

We sat in the weight of her indecision.

"Hey, you know what you can do?" Leo piped up.

"What?"

His flame grew stronger. "Let's burn Cal's letters!"

"What?! They're all I have of him!"

"You just said it yourself that these aren't him!" Leo matched her volume.

Skylar reached out to take her letters back by force, but he grabbed her hand, his tone shifting to rigid, "Learn from the past and keep it there. Trust me."

After staring at him for several seconds, Skylar's features softened. Leo released her and collected all the letters. The embers reflected in their gaze and then distinguished.

Skylar squirmed in her position, shuffling about as if that would force the words out. "I need to ask. Have you ever cried for anyone before?"

Leo fell so quiet, I didn't think he breathed. Persephone leaned closer, her eyes unblinking.

As he inhaled to speak, his sister intentionally pressed her hand against the vent floor with a lot more pressure, alerting them of our presence.

"What was that?" Skylar asked.

We shuffled out, panic seeping adrenaline into our veins.

"I don't know."

"Should we leave?"

"No, I think..."

I didn't hear the rest of their conversation as Persephone and I darted out into the hall and ran until our hearts couldn't take it any longer.

CHAPTER EIGHTEEN

A Totally Normal Patrol Through Galdor

———

Finding another secluded place, Persephone thumbed through Mr. Harris's journal and read out loud for me to be included. Entries ranged from what he gathered listening to other people's thoughts, detailed accounts of interview notes for Galdor Academy candidates, and what he knew about the AGM. Familiar names dotted the pages like Sylvia Douglas, Molly Montgomery, King Daltus, Cassius, and even mine. Though his thoughts on his own Gift were vague, earlier entries gave us hope for another possibility.

We got back to the dorm a couple of hours later.

Whispers hushed.

Fern caught my attention first, her mouth tightly closed and reminding me of when she accidentally told the others about my secret recon mission. Except this time, I was the one who was left in the dark.

"What's going on?" I demanded, looking straight at the Avlis for an answer.

Sitting on his bed, Leo replied, "We're going out."

"Out?" My face scrunched in confusion.

Kai stopped checking Leo's arm to address me directly, "Yeah, we're going on a patrol. You could use the time to clear your head."

"Then why are you acting suspicious?"

"Because we could all use time to clear our head."

"Besides, we're all a little worried for you," Fern noted.

"Fern!" Kai yelled. She jolted.

"*You* pull her away from clawing at the ceiling a day after Skylar's dad joined the Anti-Gifteds Movement."

"Can we not talk so loudly about that?" interjected Skylar.

"She didn't even take up dancing with me."

"Exactly why you need to make time," Kai noted.

"For dancing?"

"For a *patrol*, Fern. We all could use fresh air and time outside of the Grounds that isn't going to kill us."

"Dancing is still a good idea," Fern whispered.

"I'm. not. dancing." I looked from the Avlis to the Mare. "We can go on the patrol. But while we're out, we're finding Mr. Harris."

"You know where Mr. Harris is?" Molly joined the conversation. The team perked up at the sound of his name.

"We have a lead," Persephone nodded along with me. "It's still worth checking. He often wrote his entries at a bar in downtown Galdor when he first started out as a Senior Royal Crest Knight."

"After you clear your head." Kai jumped in.

I sighed at the reminder. "Did Isaac Winters at least assign us this patrol?"

"No need," Kai smiled. "Already got the Queen's permission to patrol around Galdor. She thinks you could clear your head too."

***

We weaved through the busy streets of Galdor. A group of Gifted friends laughed at their spot on the curb; an Unfortunate servant scurried past with a basket half-filled with groceries.

Leo twirled around in the streets alongside Fern. Close to one of the street stalls, I noticed him twirl and pick a peach with ease while the vendor talked with another customer. He tried handing it to me, but I conspicuously handed it to Fern who beamed at the surprise.

"You're not getting into the spirit," Leo whined.

"Go lift Molly's spirits," I suggested instead. "We're supposed to be on patrol, not stealing from civilians."

"You're *definitely* not getting into the spirit," Persephone nudged me on the other side. My shoulders pushed toward each other as they squished me. I really thought she was on my side through this.

I sighed, trudging my feet forward as the twins pressed their longer legs against mine.

"You're making her tense," objected Kai.

Skylar groaned loudly in frustration, running her hands along her face, "Just take her to the bakery!" She pointed at a bright pink sign across the street.

Fern gasped, beelining for the sweets on display.

"Good idea, Sky," Leo slapped my back with his arm and held it there. Persephone did the same, directing my shoulders toward the detour.

Skylar jolted at the sudden nickname. "You don't call me that."

"Of course, princess."

"Not—"

"Let's go, heiress."

Skylar huffed unlike a heiress and stomped behind us.

A little bell chimed as Persephone swung the door open, and we all clamored into the entranceway.

Glass displays formed a corridor, each filled with different treats and sweets ready for the taking. Persephone reached and slapped Leo's arm as his free fingers wiggled. "Quit it. We have a stipend."

"They're for the hideout," Leo encouraged.

"No."

The twins pushed me away from the door and past Kai who looked from the sweets to the drink board, whispering to himself about which combination would give him a balanced amount of sugar.

"See anything you like, Nora?" Leo asked as him and his sister moved me around the small space.

"I like," I looked at nothing of interest, "the door!" Ripping myself away from their grasp, I sprinted for the exit.

Molly moved out of the way, but Skylar forced air against my exit, keeping it shut against my best interest. Releasing the knob, I yelled at the two of them.

"Neither of you are frustrated with this ridiculous detour?"

Molly shrugged, "I don't remember the last time I had a cupcake."

"Yeah, *relax* Nora." Skylar lowered her hand. "Eat a cupcake."

"I made them at your acceptance party!" I pointed at Molly.

Molly frowned, "That was a long time ago."

Persephone restrained me again; I became more aware of how much glass surrounded us and didn't thrash.

They listed off menu items I didn't care to memorize, and I was shoved into a larger booth with pink cushions that matched the neon sign outside.

A sweet bun laid out in front of me. One bite, and I pretended to hate mine. I wouldn't give them the satisfaction or let my guard down. Skylar started an interrogation.

"So tell us more about your relationship with Prince Cassius."

I stared, silent. A meek voice overcame my desired confident one, "What brings this up?"

"You just *don't talk about him very often.*"

Oh, I see. She was mimicking me when I asked her about Cal. They still didn't know that he could hear this entire conversation.

"I talk about him all the time," I refuted.

"As the *Diviner.*" She said his title way too loudly in a public space.

Her elbow slammed into the table, and she rested her hand under her chin with a smile unrecognizable from the same ones framed in Cal's room.

"But you were *awfully* close right up till the end. You even mentioned his name and claimed he wouldn't do something so terrible to Molly's sister."

Fern's nails flexed on the edge of the table next to me.

"Some might even say you fell in love?"

Fern reached her arm out. "Enough, Skylar."

"Does that bother you, Fairaway?" Skylar feigned concern and trained her black eyes back onto me. "It sure bothers me. Were you a pet to him?"

"I wasn't—" I started but stopped myself. My fingers

rubbed against my plate.

"Then what, Nora?" Skylar egged on. "What were you to him?"

I kept my eyes down.

"What were you to him?"

My—

"His brightest Unfortunate," I murmured.

"His what?"

"Wait, no. I—" I couldn't take back my words.

"His *what?*"

"She said 'brightest Unfortunate,'" Kai said.

"I know what she said, Kai!" Skylar yelled. "What in Caliel's name does that mean?"

"I don't know," I said quickly. "I don't know."

"You better start figuring it out."

I snapped. "You better start figuring yourself out! Or are you just hoping to get on Cassius's good side when he turns you into an Unfortunate?"

It was an off-hand remark: precise in matching Skylar's cunning but careless in my disregard for her strife.

Fern stood up, her face scrunched in anger. "Enough!" she shouted. "Nora, you apologize *right now*. Skylar is your teammate. Act like it."

She turned onto the Aura. "Skylar, *you* apologize right back. You're being antagonistic for the heck of it. Nora is your teammate. Act like it."

I stared at Fern and didn't blink for several seconds. Her voice held authority, and she stood tall like an oak tree.

Skylar scoffed, "I'll apologize when she does."

I stopped myself from sighing in annoyance and maintained eye contact. "That was a careless remark. I'm sorry."

Skylar's lip wiggled along her mouth like she was about to speak but didn't want to. "I'm," she crossed her arms, "*sorry.*"

Fern clapped, bouncing back into her bubbly-self. "Great!" She grabbed my arm and pulled me out of my seat. "Now, if y'all will excuse us, none of you are helping Nora relax. So, we're going elsewhere while you find Mr. Harris."

Alarm halted me in place. "*I* want to find Mr. Harris."

"You'll get to see him when we find him," Fern countered.

"Wait, Fern!" Kai called and swayed in his seat as if he was going to stand but didn't. "The whole point—ugh—this is a disaster."

She pushed me through the entranceway and out the bakery door.

I wobbled until I successfully landed on my feet. "You know, I'm getting tired of Gifteds manhandling me."

"Then I shall walk alongside you," said Fern. We brushed sides again.

***

Fern led me to Emerald Park at the time approached six o'clock. The trees grew taller as we walked through. If I didn't hear the busy streets of Galdor not too far off from the tree line, I would think we were in Northbrook again. I understood why she would be relaxed, but why did she bring me here?

We pressed onwards until we reached a clearing. Unity flowers of red and white brightened in the late sunshine, their stems intertwined and growing together. I took a step back, horrified, thinking about Cassius sitting at the center from my dream.

"I can't be here," I whispered.

"What? Why?"

"I'm sorry." I rubbed my hands along my arms. "This just, it just makes me uncomfortable. I can't go in there."

"Oh, come on," Fern stepped into the flower bed herself and reached out to me as if that was what was scary.

"No," I shook my head violently. "I can't. I can't Fern. I can't."

Fern intertwined her hands in mine and kept us steady the way you would. Sunlight shone and warmed her touch. "How can I help you feel safe, Nora?"

I froze, contemplating my options. I could be brave. He wasn't here. It was just Fern. I trusted Fern.

"Don't let go."

Fern smiled, "I promise."

She led me forward; petals gently rubbed my ankles. My heart continued to beat dreadfully in my chest as we stood at the center of the field.

I braced for it—the moment Fern turned into Cassius, the moment I realized this was all some dream, the moment I would be his again.

Fern pulled one arm toward herself but kept her promise. My arm continued to follow as she pushed forward and switched sides. "Let's dance our worries away," she encouraged.

A nervous smile formed on my lips. "You're so insistent on that."

"Of course!" Fern's eyes expanded with her volume. "It's how we show our joy."

She spun me violently, and a cascade of flowers flung up into the air. So jarring, I couldn't help but laugh in her face as she brought me back.

"What was that?" I teased.

"Are you feeling safer?" she asked.

My smile muted but didn't disappear. "You're certainly yourself."

"Good." She released my right hand but not the other. "Can I teach you something?"

"Sure."

I followed her lead, stepping forward four steps and then backing up the same amount. We turned to each other; my feet pointed toward Fern. Connecting both hands again, we half-shuffled, half-jumped to the left without warning.

"And back!"

We half-shuffled, half-jumped to the right in easier movements.

"Now click heals."

I couldn't help but giggle as Fern tapped my ankles in unnecessarily sharp, quick movements.

"You have no idea what you're doing, do you?" I asked.

"Sometimes!" she gleefully countered.

Small misshapen flowers began to sprout and form on Fern's body and fall to the ground as she snorted. Each petal had its own unique size with colors that blended and stitched together loosely, and some were even half-formed and budding.

I watched Fern blossom and unravel, revealing herself to me.

Oh, Divine, I thought. Embarrassment continued bubbling in my throat as laughter.

Pulling our arms in any direction that kept rhythm, we danced until the sun lowered behind the tree line.

We interlocked arms and spun once more until dramatically collapsing onto a bed of unity flowers. I laid down next to her and stared upward, my face hurting from smiling.

The darkening sky wrestled between night and day, sun

and moon. Fern let out a deep sigh. "This is my favorite part of the day."

I allowed myself to sigh next to her and glanced in her direction.

"Fern?"

"Hmm?"

"You are the most consistent person in my life."

She glanced in my direction, the gravity of my words and the pink hues in the sky softening her features.

The world was a lot smaller twinkling in her eyes.

I wished we could have stayed in that lost moment for just a fraction longer.

"What are you two doing on the ground?"

Kai stood over us; the outside world tore her away from me.

We jolted and stood up. "Nothing," I said quickly. "We were just..." I looked at Fern again for one more heartbeat, "looking at the stars."

"Yeah, it was very..." Fern paused, glancing from me to Kai, "relaxing. Just what the doctor ordered. Good idea, Kai." She punched his arm, and he flinched at the sudden action.

The rest of the team revealed themselves from the darkness. "We found Mr. Harris," Leo smirked, "but we can come back later."

"No!" I shouted. "Let's go see Mr. Harris."

I've been looking forward to this for so long, I distracted myself.

"Before we go," I prompted, needing some excuse for the flush in my cheeks when Leo could see me again, "Skylar, do you want to make sure I'm not Ebony Nique?"

Though I couldn't see her eyes, her stare glared at me. "I already punched you this morning. Let's just—"

I punched her square in the face.

"*What the hell?!*" Skylar shrieked. Her face remained unchanged. Neither of us were Mutes in disguise.

"Sorry," I said. "You've just never missed an opportunity."

Persephone found me and pushed me forward while Leo found Skylar and deviated her attention from me so we could get on our way.

As the night fully took over, we scouted downtown Galdor. Lights flashed and brightened the city.

Looking up, I caught the bar's sign first, recognizing its title from Mr. Harris's writing.

Entering through the doorway, the bar was standard fare: something you could imagine anywhere, even in Thunder Bay where city guards would go in between their shifts. But there was something very special here, and he wasn't hard to find. Facing the liquor wall and head down at the bar top was Mr. Harris himself.

CHAPTER NINETEEN

Finding Mr. Harris

I couldn't believe my eyes. Frozen at the entrance, I stared at every single feature—from the slouch in his shoulders to the sunken look in his cheeks. How his wrist rotated a glass in his hand and how the brown liquid inside rotated in circles. How he was in civilian clothing that wrinkled and folded in an irregular pattern. How alive he was in simply existing but how dead his expression held, looking down into his muddled reflection.

"Would it be okay if I talked to him alone for a moment?" I asked my friends. They begrudgingly nodded one after another and obtained two tables.

I approached the bar stools.

He sighed as I grew close enough to see the grey in his hair.

"I'm not drunk." He continued to stare at the ice melting in his glass, "I can't bring myself to actually do that. I guess I still want to be at my best."

Still taken aback, all I could do was stare for a couple more moments.

"I'm so glad you're alive," I finally said.

Mr. Harris scoffed, "Can't kill me that easily." He tried to laugh, but the dryness in his throat betrayed the illusion.

"Where have you been? Queen Maya said you didn't want to be disturbed."

"I've been living as an Unfortunate." He gestured to the brand on his remaining hand. "You like what Minister Gabriel gave me?"

Disgust overtook my face. "I hate that man."

"Yeah, well," Mr. Harris took a sip of alcohol, "it's the law, isn't it?"

"I didn't come here to talk about the law." I sat down on the bar stool next to him. "You were an Animus. How?"

Mr. Harris bit his split lip. "I was never supposed to be an Animus." He stared at his glass again. "I'm the illegitimate half-brother to King Daltus. May the Divine rest his soul. My mother was a Fera, and she and our father, the late King Horace, had an affair. Would have been a lot simpler to keep their infidelity secret if I didn't carry the Animus Gift."

I allowed that information to sink in, watching how he talked about himself with the apathy of a person who didn't just confess that he was secretly a prince. A rightful king.

"But that means you *are* in the royal bloodline."

"Sure," Mr. Harris spoke doubtfully in that analysis. "But I've never really seen myself that way. After I hurt a fellow student with my Gift, I was sent back to the castle and raised to become the 1st Senior Royal Crest Knight. It's the highest position someone outside the royal line can earn. You know that."

"Did King Daltus know?"

"The only one outside our father and my mother. It's why

I had enough clearance to get you here, and why no matter what we've been through, King Daltus wouldn't remove me from my rank."

"But you were technically the true ruler of Iridion," I shook my head. "You were the most powerful Gifted in the world!"

"Now someone else is. That Gift was never meant to be mine in the first place. It's why I decided to serve the crown rather than take it the way Cassius is trying to."

We both paused, settling into silence.

Mr. Harris took another sip. "What's your next question?"

My eyes fluttered several times, trying to collect my thoughts. "There's not a lot of information on your Gift. I need to know how it works—what you can do as an Animus. If it's not...too painful."

"I hate the silence," Mr. Harris blurted.

"I'll try to think of my questions quickly then."

"No." Mr. Harris corrected flatly. "The silence."

He pointed his index fingers from side to side. "I used to hear everyone's thoughts. Everyone in this bar. I would know exactly what they were thinking at all times. And it was convenient when it needed to be."

His hands opened in a frustrated gesture. "But now it's so quiet. I have no idea what anyone is thinking anymore. I don't know how you stand it."

"I know how everyone is thinking on intuition and experience. Mrs. Montgomery would kill me otherwise," I defended. "I spent so many years pleasing the Montgomerys and the Crawfords and whomever they brought over."

"Yeah, that was one reason why I wanted you to go to Galdor." Mr. Harris's face lightened for a heartbeat. "I could read your thoughts and see all of your memories. Even the ones you tried locking away. I pushed them out and forced you to remember. Like at Molly's acceptance party."

The sudden reminder of my promise to Valerie. It wasn't raining, and yet my mind still betrayed me. Mr. Harris—Mr. Harris was right in front of me as it started happening.

"That was you?"

"Indeed. You needed a push—a reason for going."

I looked downward as my voice lowered, "I don't know if I have that push anymore."

Mr. Harris frowned but didn't share the same despair. "That's a shame. Your love for Valerie was strong. What's changed?"

I fiddled with my thumbs. "Could you read Cassius's mind?"

Mr. Harris's back straightened, "Now that boy was locked up. I could read his surface thoughts, sure, that's something I could do inherently and probably something that he can do automatically too. But he was very astute of my Gift before I knew he was. His deeper thoughts were rarely brought out around me, and when they did, they didn't make me think that he was...who he truly is."

My shoulders tensed.

"Do you know," my thumbs rotated round and round, "if he truly loved me?"

Mr. Harris finally looked directly at me. Bracing for the response, I held my breath.

"I remember his thoughts being outwardly admiring of you," Mr. Harris used his words carefully. "It was one reason why I paired you together. You both had something to prove. Both felt like you needed to be stronger."

He brought his one hand to his forehead. "I remember him liking you quite a bit, but I didn't expect you two to get so close as you did. I'm sorry."

"You had no idea," I said quickly, ignoring the loud thumping in my chest. "So, you can read people's thoughts, and you can look inside their memories. What about dreams? Did you ever insert yourself into dreams or project yourself into the waking world?"

"I experimented with dreams," he replied. "It was very difficult to practice my power within the palace walls because it would only raise suspicions. But there were a couple of times when I entered dreams. It was always fun to have that person find me the next day and tell me all about it."

Okay, so Cassius could do that, too. The confirmation was reassuring—it wasn't just my mind falling apart.

"As for projection," Mr. Harris stared off in thought, "did I add myself into someone's waking thoughts to where they could see me? No. That would have been a red flag. I'm sure I was capable. My favorite thing to do was force people to say what they were thinking. It was a great tool to get what I needed to know despite already knowing."

My arms interlocked. "That explains why I couldn't hold my tongue around you."

"No, certainly not." Mr. Harris took in a long sip. "But there were a couple of times where I didn't need to. You did that all on your own."

A small smile lightened my face for a moment before I continued. "Could you also know where people were?"

Mr. Harris squinted his eyes. "What do you mean?"

"I mean, could you connect with a person wherever you are and wherever they are and talk to them in their mind?" Divine, I sounded like a lunatic.

Mr. Harris finished his drink and signaled for another. "I could talk to people in their mind," he said. "I never considered trying to reach someone who wasn't in my line of sight. Why? Has—?"

"What about Poppy?" I interrupted his question, knowing fully that I could not answer it.

Mr. Harris leaned closer, the wrinkles in his face deepening. Even though he wasn't an Animus anymore, I still tried guarding my true thoughts.

"You met her?"

"Fought her, more like it," I scoffed. "When we were in Northbrook, the servants there said you talked to her. She's in the AGM now. Was she someone you considered for your Unfortunate project?"

"You were in Northbrook?"

"Yeah," I nodded. "Poppy was actually the one to stop me from getting to Queen Maya before...well I'm sure you've seen the Divine Observer."

"It's my only insight into what the AGM is up to now."

"What did you see in her?"

Mr. Harris paused. "A lot that I see in you."

We stared at each other, his eyes as dark as the whiskey. He squinted again, his face tightening. "Nora, has Cassius—?"

"Prince Henry is an Animus," I interrupted him again with new information, hoping that would latch onto his attention.

"Really?" Success. "Has it been confirmed?"

"Yes. Cassius saw Prince Henry's Gift when he was born, and a few days ago, he tossed a glass onto the floor while adjusting himself in his cot."

"Then there's hope for us yet." Mr. Harris's voice resonated with a new purpose.

"That's why I'm asking," I lied. "I need to know as much as I can about what an Animus can do because I imagine a baby has little to no control over that power."

"They do not, indeed," Mr. Harris made a long face,

recalling something inside himself. "That's certainly good news. We need to make sure that he's safe. When I return to the palace—"

"Mr. Harris." That fake pleasant voice of a rat chewed through my ear.

Minister Gabriel and several other large Gifteds in Royal Crest Knight uniforms approached us. His large brown eyes clawed into my skin. "And look at that. Our first Unfortunate soldier out and about. I didn't expect to see both of you together."

"Minister," Mr. Harris greeted in his usual calm voice, speaking out the names of the two other RCKs that now crowded us. "A pleasure to see you this fine evening."

"It pains me that I can't say the same," Minister Gabriel sighed, his hands behind his back and shoulders raised high. "I came to check on you. Make sure that you were well, but now I see that you are already well taken care of."

Minister Gabriel *knew* where Mr. Harris was this entire time? Any chance I could, I dug into Queen Maya to tell me where. And she told him? *Him?*

"Yes, Nora found me here," Mr. Harris defended. "It's nice to see her and the other students again."

"Yes, well I hate to do this, but it's past curfew and one of your previous students is now breaking the law."

His eyes locked onto me again. I snapped my attention to the clock near one of the TVs. 10:02pm. I was so enwrapped with finding and talking to Mr. Harris, I forgot to look at the time.

No, you're good, I reassured myself.

"But the law doesn't affect me." I pointed to Molly only two seats away. "I'm with my owner, Miss Molly Montgomery." I tried using language that would appease Minister Gabriel, but it tasted like bile in my mouth.

"Yes, well," Minister Gabriel gave me a pitiful look but with obvious relish in his face. "The law clearly states an Unfortunate servant must be with their *Gifted* owner. Miss Molly Montgomery is now an Unfortunate."

I stepped off the barstool. "You can't be serious, minister."

"That is what the law states," countered Minister Gabriel in a neutral voice I wanted to strangle, "so I have no choice but to arrest you for being a suspect of the Anti-Gifteds Movement."

As the RCKs stepped forward, my back pressed further into the bar counter.

"But I'm not part of the Anti-Gifteds Movement, minister," I appeased.

"Not part of the AGM?" Minister Gabriel raised an eyebrow. "Nora, do you want me to make an exception for one Unfortunate over another? That doesn't seem like something you would approve of."

I swallowed hard. Mr. Harris stood too, but one RCK pushed him against the counter and kept him locked in place. Even in his weakest state, he was trying to help me.

Minister Gabriel made a tsk sound. "Stand down, Peter. You're still healing. I would hate for a delay in your recovery."

That was why I hadn't seen Mr. Harris. He was the strongest opposing force to Minister Gabriel's desires. Every insult he threw at Isaac Winters would be void if Mr. Harris was back at the palace. Queen Maya would listen to him. We could stop the Diviner if those in power just listened.

"You can't keep him away forever," I said.

"I don't need to keep him away forever," the minister said. "Just long enough to get this country back on track."

Minister Gabriel's hand touched my forearm. I flinched;

water struck between us. He yelped and pulled away.

Kai brought the water back to his hand. "What would Queen Maya think, minister, if her personal guard was arrested by your hand?"

He grumbled in reply, "My dear boy, our queen isn't here. And as her spiritual advisor, I can say whatever I want that will comfort her in my decision as she's approved of before. Hasn't she, Nora?"

He stepped forward; my Gifted classmates adjusted to their stances.

"Wait!" I shot my hand out against them, my attention fixated on the minister. "Yield."

"What?" Molly spat.

"*Yield,*" I repeated. "If we fight now, we're no different from what he's accusing me of."

I hated how his lips curled along his tight face. I hated how he was right, and I certainly hated how his words sliced through me more than any weapon I could brandish.

As I stepped forward, Mr. Harris pressed closer and pulled me into a hug. He blocked Minister Gabriel's view; something tucked into my collar and hid behind my hair.

"You don't have to do this," he pleaded, unnaturally loud, like he was on stage.

I separated myself, trying to reply in a normal voice. "I'll be okay. Recover and return."

Walking over, the closest Royal Crest Knight brought me closer with his free hand. I forced myself to remain rigid and cooperative in his rough grasp. My sword disappeared from my possession, but they didn't fear me enough to check anywhere else. Gifteds never learned from their arrogance.

Nora, what's going on? Alarm drenched Cassius's speech as ice pierced up my spine with his presence.

I couldn't speak out loud as the RCK wrapped a red cloth around my mouth, and my thoughts clouded with other information. Gifteds and Unfortunates stared at me as we filed into the truck. The minister walked slowly so all those who saw me knew that I was arrested as a suspected AGM rebel.

Nora?

He pushed me inward, the truck dark and cramped.

Nora!

Cassius cursed, and I couldn't coherently respond to his plea—his thoughts jumbled with my own. Red cloth blindfolded over my eyes, and we pulled off.

CHAPTER TWENTY

He Dies Tonight

Ripping the blindfold from my eyes, the Royal Crest Knight pushed me into a crammed cell with other Unfortunates. I recognized this prison—we were beneath the palace.

"You'll stay here until your trial," Minister Gabriel said. He examined my sword instead of addressing me as though he wanted to remind me that I was without it. "Which is at an undescribed time after the Diviner conflict is over."

I pulled the red cloth out of my mouth. "You're keeping these people here forever, then."

"That's the idea." The minister locked my cell door. "If the prison gets overpopulated, we'll start thinning through the suspects."

I jumped up. "You bastard!" My body slammed into the metal bars, reaching out for his throat.

He jolted back with his eyes bulged out of his head. Recovering quickly, his face twisted in disgust.

"Don't worry," he barked, "you won't be in here for long. I'm going to make an example out of *you*."

His footsteps receded down the corridor and back up the stairs. I collapsed onto the floor, padding the back of my neck for whatever Mr. Harris gave me. I recognized its shape immediately: a small blade. Thank the Divine.

Unfortunates pressed against the walls as far away from me as possible. Looking around at the other cells, I couldn't believe Minister Gabriel detained so many of my people right below my feet. He could look me in the face at those Senior Circle meetings and relish in my ignorance all over again.

Nora! Cassius shouted so loudly in my mind, I winced and held my ear.

"You're the student, aren't you?" one of the Unfortunates asked.

I opened my eyes and looked at him from across the room. "You recognize me?"

"We all recognize you," a woman said next to me. She pulled her feet closer to her body when I looked at her. "You're the one causing trouble for the rest of us."

You're going to be okay, Nora.

"Me?" The world began to wobble and whirl.

"We might as well join the AGM," said another. I heard

him speak, but his face blurred. "Then they'd actually have a reason to arrest us."

Just hang on.

"I think my Gifted House wanted me arrested."

Eyes heavy, I blinked in slow takes. The Unfortunates around me yelled on top of each other, crying out to the Divine over our collective anguish.

"This would never happen if everyone was an Unfortunate."

"This is your fault!"

"This is..."

My feet were so worn; my cheek pressed against the cold cement. Voices drifted away—all except one so clear and urgently soft.

Just hang on.

***

My lungs contracted as if my very first breath.

I lifted my back off the ground. The prison came back into focus, and the Unfortunates around me all pressed further away in surprise.

Pressing the inside of my hand to my head, I groaned. "How...how long was I asleep?"

Eyes glanced about nervously as I awaited a response.

"We have no idea," the same disagreeable woman from before finally confessed. "Longer than you're hoping for."

Did you hear your people before your rest? Cassius asked.

My lips twitched, but I didn't respond.

Do you finally understand what I'm trying to do? For them? For you?

Shut up.

You know you should be by my side. Why are you still fighting it?

Shut up.

Look at all the people that you could free alongside me.

Shut up.

We could be free.

"I said shut up!" I finally screamed, slamming my branded hand on the ground. "Get out of my head!"

The Unfortunates around me bristled and moved closer together.

"As you wish."

I gasped, my palms flattening along the concrete. Slowly sitting on my knees and lifting my head upward, Prince Cassius stood before me. His fingers intertwined with the jail cell, looking down at me with that cheeky smile. His form suffocated any light, shrouding me in his shadow.

"Hello, Nora."

Air contracted sharply in my lungs like a knife. No. He couldn't be here. He couldn't! But the other Unfortunates trained their eyes on him too, gazing up in both awe and horror. I couldn't help but hold the same expression.

Keys appeared in his hand.

"I got here as soon as I could."

The latch audibly clicked.

"I'm glad to see you're not hurt."

He pulled the door open wide. "You're free."

Free. Relief washed over the others; the disagreeable woman sprung up and saluted him.

"Sir!" she exclaimed. "It's an honor. AGM scout Prilla at your service."

"Prilla." I watched their palms connect. I watched how marveled Unfortunate fingers reached just before his feet, how their bodies tucked tightly in a lowered position. He kept his attention on the AGM scout as if unfazed by the outward display of praise. "Is that your House name? Or your Gifted one?"

"All mine, sir!" she beamed.

"Lovely," he breathed. "Nice to see you again, Ms. Prilla. Would you help me unlock the other cells?"

"With pleasure, sir!" He handed her the keys.

Cassius bent lower to the ground, listening to the Unfortunate prayers. He placed a gentle hand on top of one of the Unfortunate women. She gasped but didn't retract. As he looked into the darkness of her Unfortunate soul, my heartbeat spiked.

"Thank you for your words. When you see the stars again, share your words with others that the Divine has delivered."

The softness in his cheeks, his lips ever so slightly separated as he breathed, the way his hair lightly shaped his face—I wanted those light blue eyes on me and see the open sky.

Cassius read my thoughts and turned, his eyes rounding and mine widening. His smile deepened.

Rising and approaching, he extended his hand. If our fingers or arms interlocked, that meant...

My hand reached out. He kept his stationary.

If your hand folded into mine, that meant...

Shaking, I was mere centimeters. A fingernail's distance.

That meant...

"Let's do this together," he said.

Sucking in a breath, I pushed up.

Just as I grazed his open palm, loud thudding erupted from above us. Footsteps, I realized, descending downwards. We all halted and stared down the hallway where the only entrance and exit was.

"She must repent and reclaim her place as a servant," Minister Gabriel's voice demanded. "If she refuses, then I must see her death firsthand. Make sure to deliver her body—"

The minister and the two Royal Crest Knights from before turned the corner and locked eyes with their captives.

Cassius lifted me from the ground and pulled me to my feet. My blood boiled.

"Planning my execution, minister?"

He glanced from me to Cassius and then back to me. His face burnt red at our hands, at our position side by side.

"Kill all prisoners who are already out of their cells and capture the prince! My boy, you need redemption, too."

Cassius scoffed, a shadow crossing over his face. "Never talk to me about the Divine's word, minister. It doesn't suit you."

Minister Gabriel inhaled, his eyes piercing. "Whoever brings me the Unfortunate soldier's body will earn my favor."

The two Royal Crest Knights readied; the Unfortunates and I bristled.

Cassius placed his hands in his pockets. "Whoever takes a step forward will become an Unfortunate body and will earn my disfavor."

The Gifted on the left of Minister Gabriel stepped forward. But the RCK halted as he tried throwing a punch, frozen mid-air. I knew that feeling all too well—to have complete understanding of your surroundings without control or autonomy.

The Diviner reached out and pressed his thumb against the RCK's forehead. "I don't have many Feras. Your sacrifice will not be in vain."

The RCK tried to strain but only created incoherent sounds out of a closed mouth.

If you can see it with the mind of your heart, and feel it in the depths of your soul, then you will hold it in your hands, Cassius repeated those words in my mind.

Bright hues of red and white filled the enclosed space, reminding me of Molly's Gift condensed in a marble.

From my position, movement caught my attention. The other Royal Crest Knight was not struck in awe as the Unfortunates were; he lunged forward.

I sidestepped. A knife plunged into the Gifted's throat; he collapsed immediately, gasping for air and choking on his blood. The knife was no longer behind my back. Had I....had I just...?

Those blue eyes fixated on me, and the Royal Crest Knight in front of him dropped dead on the floor too. He pocketed the marble from the first assailant, but we continued to stare. What do you say when you save your greatest enemy?

Minister Gabriel heaved in a fearful breath, losing balance and falling onto one of the cell doors. He found enough momentum to race back up the stairs. What if he wasn't my greatest enemy?

Grabbing Cassius's forearm, I stopped him from whatever hell he was about to unleash.

"I'll go after him," I said.

Cassius stared at my hand pressed tightly against the leather of his sleeve. Inhaling deeply, his attention moved to my face so close to his.

"I'll lead the Unfortunates to safety and cover you."

Releasing my hold, I nodded and charged up the stairs after the minister. I saw him, fumbling and crying as he fled.

Pushing the doorway back into the palace, he pointed downwards. The two Royal Crest Knights who guarded the entranceway peered in and saw me; I halted as they blocked my path.

But Cassius kept true to his word. One look and they collapsed, their skulls audibly splitting before they hit the floor.

I continued on, chasing the minister down the corridor and to his chambers.

He dies tonight!

I burst through the door he flung closed.

Minister Gabriel hunched over in the corner of his office, cowering below me. Absolutely pathetic. Tears swelled in his large, authoritarian eyes. Now it was his turn to dwell in fear—to understand what it meant to be under another's mercy.

And I didn't have any.

I found my sword on the desk. Reclaiming my weapon, I stepped in his direction and toward the window to his right.

Swinging my sword with one hand, the glass shattered, cascading to the floor like rain. Minister Gabriel shouted, covering his head as smaller fragments broke apart around him. I sheathed the sword, bending downwards.

"What are you doing? You get away from me!" he demanded. Shards glistened between my fingers.

The minister pulled closer to the wall as we made eye contact. He gasped, flailing about as he tried and failed to back away. This was the Gifted who tormented me? The one who could convince others to throw me in jail and persuade the Senior Circle to follow his desires?

Pieces of glass bled his palm, reminding me of his mortality.

I stepped forward, my jaw tightened and heart beating rapidly in my chest. He yelled at me again, his voice high-pitched and desperate.

Grabbing his collar, I pulled him close and forced glass into his eyes. The minister's scream drilled into my ears; blood poured down his cheeks.

I pushed him away from me. He slammed onto the ground, disoriented and helpless.

A Lux was no different from an Unfortunate without his eyesight.

I stepped over to the kindling fireplace, his screams becoming background noise. Lifting the U-shaped rod from the flames, it reminded me of a bo staff. A familiar weapon.

Red and orange hue reflected in my stare.

I approached the minister. He heard my footsteps along the wooden floor.

"What? What are you doing?!"

"Under the seventh law of servitude," I began.

He pushed himself against the wall again, throwing whatever he could cling onto. Books and papers and pens cascaded the floor without any direction.

I advanced.

"All Unfortunates are required to wear a brand on the back of their dominant hand."

He kept rambling, pleading for his life to a higher power who only watched.

"Which is your dominant hand, minister?" I bellowed.

I didn't wait for a response, plunging the iron onto his forehead. The stench of seared flesh invaded my senses. The rod sank deeper into his body, tearing apart the muscles underneath, and marking him equal to me. I kept the rod steady as the rest of his body convulsed.

I didn't realize that Minister Gabriel stopped screaming until I finally released my hold.

The rod crashed to the floor as I caught a glimpse of my actions. The minister's neck bent upwards, his eyes bloodshot, open, and unblinking. His lungs didn't contract; his expression stayed frozen in agony.

I expected that icy feeling up my spine—entangled to the Diviner's command. But my entire body burned hot and ragged; I was fully in control of my actions.

Huffing, I heard the floor creak behind me. I turned sharply; Cassius stood in the doorway. Disbelief overcame his usual certainty.

As my voice hitched, the prince raced forward. His arms wrapped around my frame. I didn't draw away, leaning closer into his embrace.

"It's okay," the prince assured in a soft voice. "It's okay. He can't hurt us anymore."

My face buried in his chest, shaking uncontrollably. It was over. How many Unfortunates did I save by killing the monster?

Prince Cassius held me tighter.

You saved so many, his voice wrapped around my panicked thoughts like a blanket. *They're safe and with my people. They're all safe because of us.*

His lips pressed against my forehead. I turned upwards to meet his face. Cassius looked as he did when we first danced together—when we first kissed. His mouth twitched as he read my thoughts, but I didn't care. I leaned upwards; he leaned downwards. Our lips connected.

We pressed into each other, my thoughts blurring and my heart beating with his. We stayed locked onto each other. He directed my shoulders to the left wall and pinned me there with his knee, one hand securely wrapped around my frame and the other holding my head up to him. My left hand cupped his jawline, keeping him closer to me.

We continued to kiss, light puffs brushing against my

cheek as he panted. I lost breath too.

You're back to me.

Was that his thought or mine?

He pressed me harder against the wall; our kisses became more desperate.

A static of thunder prickled the back of my neck. I halted, remembering the hand I held.

Cassius's smile shifted to concern. "No, no. Nora, stay with me."

The same plea I said to him at the Determination. Before he revealed himself as the Diviner. Why did you have to be one in the same? Why do you make me wish I could stay?

"Then stay!" Cassius urged, pressing his forehead to mine. His blue eyes suffocated my vision; both hands clasped with mine, his bracelet grazing my wrist. "We're capable of changing the world together."

"But you're the Diviner."

"And you downcasted the Divine's false mouthpiece."

Minister Gabriel laid dead to my right.

I swallowed hard, looking back to Cassius. "That's different."

"You can't lie to me, Nora."

He placed his thumb on my chin, leaning close and his eyes half-closed. Thunder crashed overhead, snapping me out of my desires.

I flinched, recoiling away on instinct. The prince held me there. "If you come with me, you'd never fear the rain again."

"I—"

Clanking metal and approaching footsteps denoted guards.

Cassius and I locked eyes. "Nora, come back with me. Of your own choice."

My voice hitched in my throat. I could now hear the guards

shouting orders, their voices jumbled together.

My heart tore in two directions. We couldn't be seen together again. Not like this. My choice dwindled with each heartbeat.

Cassius exhaled a deep sigh as I frantically looked to the doorway.

Until I hold you again, my Unfortunate.

I turned back to an emptiness in front of me. Wind rustled through the broken window.

"Nora!" I flinched at the sound of my name, turning to see Isaac Winters leading a charge of other Royal Crest Knights. He glanced from me to Minister Gabriel's body to me again. "What happened?"

I stared at the window for several seconds pondering the what-ifs…

Shakily, I finally said, "The Diviner was here."

I woke to something in bed with me, restraining my arms.

Panic seeped into my heart until I noticed a tuff of blond hair amidst the sheets. Cassius held my shaking body, his blue eyes filled with concern.

"It's okay Nora. You're okay."

Taking in a few deep breaths, I struggled between rapid heartbeats. Was this real? Was he really in bed with me?

"What happened?" I whimpered.

His hand pressed against my forehead. "You were having a nightmare." He adjusted the blankets and tucked me in. Was I really having a nightmare? I didn't remember.

Cassius rubbed my back, whispering, "Relax. Go back to sleep." Eyes heavy, I rested my head back on the pillow facing him.

I sank.

And sank.

The bed fell away, and I sank in a dense, inky abyss. Void of light, of life, of myself. Closing my eyes, I sank further.

The density fell away, and I opened my eyes to twinkles— first sparse and then abundant. I sank in an airy night sky. My body titled as I outstretched my arm, reaching for the Divine's hand to save me.

I sank further.

Until the darkness was interrupted by the brimming of

light and a large city off in the distance. The Iridion Castle stood proudly at the center.

Slowly, my toes reached the ground and I stood on a porch. Cassius came out of the house, wrapping his arms securely around my smaller frame. He leaned closer and rested his chin on my shoulder, leaning towards my neck.

We watched the sunrise.

Red brightened the horizon and filled each building. Except the sun flickered in raging movements, the night sky no longer held stars, and Galdor's skyline crumbled before us.

Fire reflected in my pooling eyes. What is this?

My chest burned as Cassius said, *This is what you choose.*

CHAPTER TWENTY-ONE

(Un)Trustful

———

Waking with a jolt, darkness stared right back through the gap in the ceiling.

Sitting at Queen Maya's desk as she ordered Gifteds and Unfortunates alike, I continued to think about him.

My fingers gripped the pencil as I wrote a letter to Valerie. Seamlessly, too. I should have been proud to write something without thinking about it. But I wasn't thinking about my writing.

I was thinking about his lips pressed against mine as Queen Maya listed off her favorite finger foods and colored drinks and his eyes so intensely gentle as the queen debated if a pink color scheme matched with marble more than gold. She worried about dresses and which one she should wear that would show the most regalia, and she discussed what the Royal Crest Knights should wear versus the Senior members. She gave Mercy agency and asked what the Unfortunate servants should wear in rotation and what music they should practice that matched the selected dances. She managed the list of guests: who was coming, who would sit next to who and who needed to be far away from each other, their excuse of absence, and whether or not to send flowers from the ball or from a separate bouquet. And she coordinated security with Isaac Winters, scaling the guest vs servant ratio in the Gifteds favor and deciding which Unfortunates were loyal to the crown based on their time working in the castle.

All background noise to my what-ifs. What if I chose to go with Cassius? What would Queen Maya think of me? What would my friends think like Fern, Kai, Leo, Persephone, and Molly? Would Skylar feel vindicated? It was easier to prove Minister Gabriel right about me than to my classmates.

But what if I had gone? He treated us as equals—the way I and so many others wanted to be treated. I couldn't ignore that, but he hadn't reached me since the dream, and that realization sliced deeper than any blade.

My hand stopped moving along the page. This wasn't a letter to Valerie anymore.

Huffing, I ripped the page out. The crinkle brought Queen Maya's attention to me. I stared back at those blue eyes she shared with her brother. But I didn't see the open sky or an abyss or an ocean. I saw dewdrops, two dull gems that matched the shape of her earrings.

Could I really let his sister destroy herself like this? I had to warn her again. My conscious couldn't rest.

"Your Majesty," I twirled the pencil in my hand.

"Yes Nora, what is it?"

I adjusted in my seat several times, building up the courage to confront her once more.

"I can't deny that I saw Cassius, Your Highness. I really think we should stop this ball before it begins. We have no idea what he's planning with such an event."

Queen Maya waved her hand at me as if I just told her an inconvenience rather than a threat to her power. "I understand that you're stressed after seeing Minister Gabriel die, but I wouldn't worry."

"*Worry?*" Alarm raised my voice an octave. "He was here in the castle walls! He has access to the castle somehow! You don't deny that I saw him, but you insist there is no reason to worry? Why are you not worried, Your Majesty?"

"Nora, that is enough."

I wanted to shout; I wanted to scream in hopes that she would listen. But knowing how thin her patience grew lately or how recently she forced me to bow to her against my desires, I didn't. I needed a new approach.

"Why do you want this ball so badly, Your Majesty?" I lowered my voice. "What do you hope to gain?"

"I keep remembering a ball we held when I was..." she stumbled to find the right word, "younger, and how that brought the kingdom closer. How alliances and friendships and reunions strengthened amidst the dancing."

Dancing. I stopped myself from rolling my eyes at another mention of dancing.

As Queen Maya spoke, her eyes drifted far away as though to a memory and a gentle smile warmed her face and reminded me of when we first met. So much had changed between us and within herself since then.

She finally looked at me in the face. "I still believe everyone has the ability to do good and to be given second chances. Surely I should give that courtesy to myself."

We stared at each other for several heartbeats. I retreated back to my paper with a despondent look.

In the moment, the consequences of killing Minister

Gabriel were irrelevant to me. But after I claimed that the Diviner had killed him instead, alongside freeing the castle Unfortunate prisoners, I expected Queen Maya to react differently. I expected her to react rationally—maybe even irrationally in the opposite direction. But not this.

Queen Maya walked toward me. Her face softened as her gloved hand reached out towards mine on the desk. I watched as her hand hovered like when I reached out to Cassius. I watched her struggle.

"I am still unable to reach even you," she sniffled, pulling her hand back to her chest. She sighed and stared at my bare hands, her voice drifting away as if she talked to herself. "Not yet."

She straightened back to attention and returned to planning. As I went back to writing, Mercy came over and sat down next to me.

"Would you like to take him?"

I looked down to Prince Henry. "What?"

"My arms are getting tired. Would you mind taking him for me?"

"Oh," I paused, "sure." I reached my arms out and accepted the baby in hand. He was getting heavier and older. More tufts of blond hair formed on his head as if overnight.

Prince Henry was kidnapped once before by Ebony Nique. If I accepted Cassius's hand and ran away with him, would I kidnap his baby brother too? Would I hand Prince Henry over to the Diviner and watch as his Gift tore away? The act would surely kill him as it had with nearly all the others.

"Mercy?"

"Hmm?" The Unfortunate servant tilted her head.

"What do you really think of this ball?" I leaned closer so the queen couldn't hear. "You've said yes to everything Maya has suggested, but you must know how ridiculous it all is.”

Mercy blinked rapidly, her only indication that she was processing how to respond. “I cannot openly speak out against the queen.”

“Yes, but if you could,” I urged.

“What, like you?” Mercy’s caution shifted into one of resolve.

My own eyes widened at the scathing comment.

She continued in a harsh whisper, “Unfortunates don’t get the same privilege to voice their opinion like you do. And so carelessly at that. You forget what it means to be an Unfortunate—tiptoeing around hostility and violence and apathy at all times instead of the one who inflicts it. It takes years to perfect.”

“I’m aware.”

“Are you?” Mercy challenged, the light refracting and darkening her skin tone. “You don’t have that sad little look in your eyes. So intense, like those in the Anti-Gifteds Movement, but you get away with it because you play the pet. You’re the model Unfortunate for Gifteds rather than your own people.”

I stared at Mercy, unsure how to respond. Where did this come from? She spat in my face, echoing my own fears and reminding me of Sylvia Douglas and Poppy and the directionless Fairaway servants and the arrested AGM Unfortunate who named herself Prilla and all the Unfortunates I killed or found dead at Galdor Square and all the Unfortunate girls in tacky, lavish outfits dampened by the rain and the Unfortunate whose unbreakable promise led me here in the first place, Valerie.

Like Divine intervention.

I looked back at Queen Maya, giddily planning her own

ruin. I needed to get out of this room.

"Excuse me." I handed the baby back to Mercy.

Queen Maya glanced in my direction as I left but didn't say anything. The door clicked softly behind me. I didn't know where I should go. If there was nothing I could do to stop this ridiculous ball...then maybe I could at least prepare.

I didn't make it five steps before Kai intercepted.

Raising an eyebrow, I watched him walk next to me. "Were you waiting for me?"

"I wasn't sure when your session would be over," he admitted.

Kai knew well enough that he could always talk to me during lunch or dinner. He wouldn't usually waste time when fixed ones were already in place.

"It's over. What's wrong?"

Kai reached out and grabbed my shoulders, stopping me in place. He glanced around to the empty hallway and whispered,

"The real reason I had us go on a patrol was to ask you something critical. If Skylar didn't twist our intentions, then I could have asked you sooner. But between finding Mr. Harris and learning of Minister Gabriel's death—"

"What happened with Mr. Harris after I was," I paused, "arrested?"

"He became so frustrated with himself that he left. There wasn't much he could do, but he did give us an address."

Kai pulled out a small piece of paper, but when I tried receiving it for myself, he pushed it back into his pocket with his fingers still pinched along the folds.

"Nora." He kept his eyes on the ground for a moment.

I brought my hands to my chest. "What's wrong, Kai?"

"We're thankful for your silence with Skylar, and Molly is grateful for your help with her little sister and with herself.

And I'm really glad we all spent time together in Northbrook before the AGM ruined it, and though I didn't make it through the Simulation Lab as much as I should have, Fern told me all the ways you tried sacrificing yourself in that impossible scenario."

He looked at me, his fragile voice continued, "And we're all so glad that you were released from prison, too, but...we're also so worried about you. No one knows what happened. We can only go off your word. But if you're telling the truth, that means the Diviner freed you from that jail cell."

I froze, my heart sinking.

"It means you saw him again. It means you two were together until Isaac Winters found you alone, practically unscathed, with Minister Gabriel's body. So, I need to ask you, Nora..."

My throat tightened; my breathing shortened.

"Can we trust you to still be our leader?"

INTERLUDE 6

That night, I slept as you did beneath the earth—still and uninterrupted within the voided darkness.

Untethered to any imagery or sound or distraction.

Cassius gave me the dark, so all I could do was unravel my thoughts, string together all my what-ifs, and decide if I was a leader for my Gifted friends or a leader alongside the Diviner. If my place at Galdor Academy could still make a difference or if I was supposed to reject Mr. Harris when he proposed such a ridiculous idea. If Valerie would approve of how I've kept our promise or if there was still more promise to keep.

If I could help all Unfortunates escape servitude, where was I meant to be?

CHAPTER TWENTY-TWO

The Decision

—

The ball began: lavish, bright, and all-consuming.

At the center stood Queen Maya, so intensely radiant with each step and alit by the flashing cameras that I could barely make out her features. Her smile blurred in and out of focus behind the wave of her gloved hand, and when her lips moved, the small audience around her smiled back.

Obscured by her form, Mercy and I walked behind her. She appeared as a capable leader—so foreign a concept now as we ascended the stairs to the throne along the left side of the ballroom opposite the entranceway.

Mercy leaned into my ear, whispering, "I need to help guests in. Excuse me."

She bowed before walking out of sight. That's right—that was her job tonight. Prince Henry was close by but in a separate room with Persephone and other Gifted elite. They were past the exit to my immediate right. After the Determination, I understood why no Unfortunate was allowed to take care of him during such an important event. At least Queen Maya learned something while repeating history.

Three thrones lined the platform. The queen sat in the central chair. Isaac Winters and I remained standing behind her. Minister Gabriel would have replaced Isaac on her left side if I hadn't killed him. But we adjusted accordingly, and questions regarding his murder were waved off by the queen.

Tonight is about uplifting the country and bringing us all together again, she repeated in various ways. *A regional minister would take Gabriel's place soon after.*

I stood at Queen Maya's right as her personal guard, a title she assigned me after the Determination. I said it wasn't enough to be Iridion's first Unfortunate soldier. I still believed that. But in which direction...I didn't sleep well last night trying to muster a true answer.

The party started. Guests arrived at the platform lower than the one we stood on now. After announced by a man in a black and white suit, the Gifteds bowed to their queen from a distance and descended to the main floor, their heads lowered as they stepped down.

Royal Crest Knights and even some third-year students lined both walls. To my left, Fern and Kai were stationed at the end of the buffet. So close to the dessert bar, Kai kept Fern's appetite in check so she wouldn't become distracted.

To my right, a small band of Unfortunates played string music, their hands more shaky due to the guards who surrounded them. An invisible circle condensed the dancers along the polished floor. Conversing guests, security guards, photographers, and servants holding specialty trays all lined the outer ring of the ballroom.

Leo and Skylar paralleled each other and circled the dance floor, observing each person who crossed their path. Molly stood directly next to the kitchen door to my left, scanning every servant who scurried in and out as they attended to the buffet and guest needs.

"Your Majesty?" I prompted. "Permission to supervise the Unfortunate staff." It was my responsibility as the default head servant to the Montgomery House when Molly held her acceptance party. When Mr. Harris invited me to Galdor Academy. If I could be inside, then maybe...

The queen waved her hand, "Oh, don't mind that, Nora. I want you right here." She gestured to where I stood and then turned to look at me, her head resting on her hands and eyes sparkling against the chandelier. She looked more like an excited child than a ruler who could be overthrown this very night.

I recognized that smile from one of my nightmares—the one where Cassius and I danced in a ballroom. Looking around, purple replaced gold but the walls were still marbled. Trained Unfortunate servants moved their arms in rhythmic movements, and Gifteds in dazzling dresses floated as they spun.

Cassius and I danced in *this* ballroom. It couldn't have been a vision of where he was in the present; the queen was noticeably younger than she was now. So what could it mean?

Calm down, I urged myself. I could see the entire room from where I stood; nothing could slip past me.

"I'll stay next to you the whole night, Your Majesty," I said quickly. Even if Maya couldn't stop Cassius as a capable ruler, I still wanted to protect *her*.

"Excellent!" the queen clapped her hands.

The party continued. Guests arrived at the platform. After announced, they bowed to the queen and descended to the main floor. Royal Crest Knight uniforms mixed with academy student uniforms. Fern and Kai moved up and down the buffet line and then remained stationary again. The orchestra continued to play, each song moving effortlessly into the other. Leo and Skylar circled each other with the cameras, the guards, and the guests. Molly remained still next to the kitchen door. Gifteds danced and ate and danced some more. The buffet never emptied.

The party continued. Stragglers arrived at the platform, were announced, and bowed their heads. Uniforms decorated the dance floor in the same three colors. Fern, Kai, and Molly stood; Leo and Skylar circled side by side. Gifteds danced and chatted and stared. They'd condense in really small circles, huddled and crammed, and turn their necks up at their queen.

Their eyes drifted over to me, noticed my returning glare, and immediately looked down. Sipping wine or fiddling with their food without actually eating made for a purposeful distraction as they tried to appear normal. All acting like Unfortunates caught doing something impolite.

I watched as they separated and came back together again, intermixing with others and sometimes regrouping with the same socialites.

Mr. Stanton arrived at the platform. He stared up at us; I couldn't read his face well past a fake smile. He was announced. He bowed and descended into the ballroom. He acknowledged his daughter but did not linger, mixing in and out of unheard conversations and comments.

The party continued. Fern and Kai were there. Molly was there. And Leo and Skylar were nearby, too. Mercy arrived with a large plate of fruits, cheese squares, meat slices, and precisely-decorated candies for the queen.

"Nora."

"Hmm?"

Queen Maya looked at me with the same relish she gave a pink cupcake. "I want to see you dance."

That was certainly a weird request. "Are you feeling well, ma'am?"

"Never better, Nora. I'll feel even better when I see you dance."

I held back my muscles from involuntarily twitching, "With whom, ma'am?"

The queen sighed, "I would love to but that's not feasible yet. No. Let's get someone else."

I looked over to Fern.

"Mercy." Queen Maya gestured to the Unfortunate servant.

We looked at each other, both our eyebrows raised. I forced my words out, "Very well, ma'am."

Linking our arms, we descended the stairs. Isaac Winters was with the queen. She would be safe until my return. She would be safe.

I've eaten those words before.

Skylar nudged Leo, and they noticed us. I didn't blink as I stared at them—my way of letting them know that I was here and they needed to be more alert than ever.

"Would you like to lead first?" Mercy asked.

"It doesn't matter," I replied.

We loosely held each other, both obligated by Queen Maya's attentive stare. That was her way of dancing, I supposed. To watch others and imagine herself in that scenario. Why did it have to be me?

I looked beyond Mercy, but we moved too quickly to see anything useful. Eyes brought a trickle down my back as the Gifteds around us stared. In the split seconds my body stilled, I could see their tightly concentrated faces as they masked their true feelings from me. All like Unfortunates at a

Choosing Ceremony.

"People are staring," I cautiously whispered.

"Pay them no mind," Mercy assured, shifting her hand up.

"Yes, but..." I spun, continuing to glance about the guests.

"Turn your eyes on me."

My hands fell back into Cassius's palms.

I gasped.

The music abruptly ended; everyone stopped moving all together; their faces turned to us. My friends saw us connected.

Time stood as still as we did, our breaths held and eyes wide. All frozen as if under his stolen Animus Gift. Cassius relished in my shock.

I wanted to stay in that momentary pause the way we all had for so long. Standing, unmoving, unraveling. But our time waiting for Cassius's return ran out, and he was once more in front of the world. Right in front of me.

Withdrawing from his touch, I screamed, "It's the Diviner! Run! Secure the queen!"

I looked to the Gifted guests and the Royal Crest Knights along the wall and the servants and reporters and fixated cameras. They all remained stationary.

"Cassius, release them from your control." I turned to him.

"They're not under my control." Cassius leaned in and softly pressed his lips against my forehead. "They're under my command."

Feet shifted behind me. I turned back as the Gifteds around us separated into two parallel lines. So fearful to keep their Gifts—they would do anything. Mr. Stanton's change in loyalty was now inside the heart of Iridion. How could I see it too late?

Mr. Stanton restrained Mercy even though she moved in unison, keeping her in front of him and in my sight. I glanced to where my friends were when I last saw them. Though they all remained still in place, their frozen expressions of horror, alarm, and disgust brought tears to my eyes.

This isn't what I wanted. Not the promise I wanted to fulfill.

The Gifted stopped, forming a pathway directly to Queen Maya. Directly to the throne.

Isaac Winters had taken several steps forward but remained frozen in place mid-stride, his hand held out in front of him but no ice appeared. Maya was completely defenseless.

She peered down at her brother from the top of the staircase just as she had in my dream—only now she was a queen instead of a princess. Only now, this wasn't their first reunion.

"The first time I got to see my brother—or at least remember seeing him—was at my 14th birthday party. He had ran off for doing something unfavorable...when I was a baby and he was six years old."

Why was I remembering this conversation now?

"But he came back as a birthday present to me. I had never been so happy before in my life."

He came back. He came back. He came back... Her words replayed and overlaid in my subconscious.

I had forgotten. Now, I couldn't get it out of my head. When Cassius and I danced in that dream...it was when he came back on her 14th birthday. The smile she had then—it was the same damn smile she had during the ball, anxious for his arrival.

I blinked back into the present.

Queen Maya raced down the stairs.

"I knew you would come," she breathed a sigh of relief and knelt down before her brother. "And I didn't forget what you told me at the Determination. You didn't take the throne then because you said I'd hand it to you. Well, you were right, so here!"

She pulled the crown off her head and offered it to him.

"Take it! Take it all from me. No one is on my side anymore. I could never reach my people—Gifted or Unfortunate. I'm not meant to be their leader."

Cassius stared at the crown between his sister's gloved fingers. "You defile the Gift granted to you with open palms. Your desires will be fulfilled."

Desires? What was he getting at? But one look back at Kai and that question no longer was at the forefront of my mind. I wanted to be a leader worthy of them. And I failed time and time again. I wouldn't this time.

"You got what you want," I said. "Now release my friends."

Cassius spoke slowly, "You still deny me?"

I heard Fern scream first. Kai collapsed next to her. Leo and Skylar and Molly all fell away from my sight, but their desperation filled the ballroom and echoed off the walls.

"Yes, I choose them!" I yelled and grabbed ahold of his wrist. "Now stop!"

Their shrieks grew louder. Their bodies thrashed and curled.

"Cassius, stop!"

He raised his free hand, and their pain no longer pierced my ears. My friends coughed and wheezed and gasped but they were alive and began standing on their own.

Cassius stared through me. "By God, you're bright."

"Cas," Maya said. His attention drifted to her. She swallowed hard before continuing, "you promised no harm would befall my subjects."

"They sow their own demise." His voice was despondent. I

stared into the night sky as his eyes turned back to me. "Do what you will. There will be consequences."

The Gifted line parted for me as I ran over to Fern.

I reached for her hand. "We're retreating with Prince Henry."

Kai positioned himself in a defensive stance. I didn't blame him.

"I haven't been a leader worth trusting," I admitted, "so *please*, let me make that up to you now."

After several heartbeats, Fern grabbed my hand and the two of them followed me toward the others.

I grabbed ahold of Skylar's hand before she could attack. "We're retreating with Prince Henry."

The Aura kept her eyes on Cassius. "I need to save my father."

Her father stood in the line of Gifteds. "He's made his choice. What about you, Skylar?"

We struggled wordlessly against each other. She ignored my question. "Why are you stopping me?"

"Because you're my friend!" I looked at Molly and then back to Skylar. "At least you have the capacity to be."

Leo grabbed ahold of her other hand before she could argue further. The wind settled, and we retreated to the one exit that would take us to Persephone—in a secret room alongside the young prince.

Mercy, released from her hold, following us through the second smaller ballroom and down another exit that led to a corridor.

If Cassius brought the Anti-Gifteds Movement, they weren't here yet. We still had a chance. I locked onto the third door at the end.

Knocking the pattern with quick precision, the door

creaked open ajar. I bolted inward. Persephone already held the baby in her arms.

"We need to go," I said.

She nodded. I looked to the Royal Crest Knights, unsure of their true loyalty "Cassius has taken over. Either submit to him or flee yourself."

They looked at me and then at the other Unfortunate. We rushed out before they responded. As long as they didn't follow us, I didn't care for their answer.

"I can hold him if you like," offered Mercy.

She reached for the child, but Persephone kept him close. "I got him."

Mercy frowned; we kept going. The sound of commotion halted us in place. AGM rebels were nearby. The walls leaned inwards; the cracks all around us deepened. I couldn't risk turning another corridor. Our luck would eventually run out.

Turning toward the row of long rectangular windows, I swung my sword against the glass. It shattered, cascading in pieces along the foundation below our feet.

"Fern," I begged, "help me."

She came closer. The distance to the ground expanded as we peered down. Dusting off glass, she placed her palms on the railing and closed her eyes. Several seconds passed before the grass so far below us began to pull and twist upwards. A small stalk cemented itself to the castle's wall.

"Go," I demanded.

One after the other, my team lifted themselves out the window and down the makeshift ladder. First Molly. Then Kai.

"Let me help you," Mercy offered again but Persephone refused.

Then Persephone with Prince Henry. Then Leo. Then Skylar.

"Okay, Fern. Your turn."

My heart raced louder the more the AGM neared. If they caught us now... I couldn't think about that possibility.

Fern jumped onto the ledge and lowered herself until she found her footing. Sheathing my sword, I held her hand, though I was sure she anchored me more than I anchored her. She looked at me expectantly, as if I would go next.

"I'll be right down," I assured her.

She paused and nodded weakly.

Her hand grazed my fingertips; my body tore away in a sharp motion as hands wrapped around my frame. My lungs sank into a short gasp; Fern managed to latch onto my right arm.

How did they catch me?

"If I can't hand over the baby," Mercy's voice overlaid with another—one that shifted into mine before—and revealed herself as a Mute whose done this her entire life. Ebony Nique pulled me close to her, "then I'll hand over you!"

"Nora!" Fern's hands fell from my arm to my wrist.

I reached for my sword, but Ebony pressed my hand down. We fought over the handle and forced a stalemate.

Fern looked down, the veins of her arms and her neck protruding as she shifted the earth below her.

But movement caught the corner of my eye. Both ends of the hallway filled with red-marked soldiers. I was done for.

As I looked past Fern to the wall they had to scale, the same daunting wall so pristine when I first arrived at Galdor Academy, figures shrouded in shadow began to swarm and narrow my friends' escape.

The Diviner's presence weaved his way up my spine. It wasn't too late for them.

"Let go."

"What?"

I looked directly at Fern. "They can't capture you too."

Fern shook her head, her voice firm. "No."

"Protect each other."

"Nora!"

"Protect all you can: Gifteds and Unfortunates."

"Nora!" Her hands fell from my wrist to my palm.

"Can you promise me that?"

When she didn't respond, I urged her. "Can you promise me that?"

"Yes!" she yelled, "Yes. I promise!"

Giving her a pained smile, I relaxed my fingers and fell away from the people I cared about most. She screamed my name. I was all too familiar with that sorrowful shriek—the way I screamed your name too.

I watched the freedom we hoped for fall out of my hands for a second time as Ebony locked my arms together behind me. So this is how it felt, Valerie. I'm so sorry I couldn't be there for you. I'm so sorry I couldn't be there.

Ebony yanked me away from the window as my friends ran toward the wall, toward the ever-pooling number of Anti-Gifted soldiers. I didn't see them engage. I didn't see them escape.

But I had to believe they did. She promised me.

CHAPTER TWENTY-THREE

The Dark Blue Coloring of the World

Thrown back into the ballroom, I could witness for myself that all of Maya's meticulous planning fell away. Soldiers dressed in servant attire removed the decorations they placed there not one day earlier. Soldiers adorned in red barricaded the Royal Crest Knights on the left side of the room and guarded the

Gifted guests along the right. Both detained groups sat with their heads down, though the Royal Crest Knights faced the wall with their assailants facing their backs. Only the guests whispered among themselves.

Cassius stood at the base of the staircase, giving orders to other AGM soldiers. Several Unfortunates forcefully brought him a Gifted man from the right side—one of the men who switched sides as Mr. Stanton did.

Cassius said something I couldn't hear but it brought the Gifted man to tears.

He ignited his arms into flame and burned the Unfortunates around him, but Cassius narrowed his eyes and the man became so still, he couldn't use his Gift anymore. The flames suffocated, and then the man perished as Cassius pressed his fingers to his forehead.

A marble illuminated in an orange hue; the man collapsed and didn't move.

Many others laid out on the floor as if discarded from their usefulness, stripped of all power and life. Isaac Winters was not among them.

A familiar face strained while dragging another older man behind her. Blood and pieces of his flesh stuck to the floor. She saw me and released his legs, running up and waving at me like an old friend.

"Glad to see you again," Poppy smiled, glancing from me to Ebony right behind my head. "See the bodyguard has a bodyguard. You can be released, Ebony! She won't run with me here, right?"

Poppy looked at me expectantly, but all I could do was stare at how tall she was. She reminded me too much of Fern, of an Avlis.

"I think Cassius took care of that," I replied in a dry voice.

"Very good," Poppy didn't miss a beat and wrapped her arm behind my neck. This was the same girl who stopped me from reaching Maya at the Flower Festival and then attacked me again while rescuing Melanie. Didn't she blame me for her friends' deaths? From the way she gleamed, it was like none of that ever happened.

She walked me past the dead man and toward Cassius.

Maybe she was cheerful because he won. Her friends didn't die in vain.

I prayed mine didn't either.

I looked up to the grand chandelier and watched how its jewels twinkled—each so glimmering I had to squint my eyes. Lowering my gaze to the center of the ballroom, I noticed a crumbled figure on the floor, her hair matted and her dress clinging tightly to her panting body.

"Maya!" I called her name, alerting Cassius to my voice. Forcing Poppy off me, I ran to her. Fear overtook my anger, and my hand reached out, ready to lift her up, when I noticed her gloves were missing. I stopped and hesitated.

Cassius and I towered over his sister.

"What did you do to her?" I demanded.

"I gave her what she always wanted."

"What she always wanted? What could—?"

Her bare hand wrapped around mine. A sharp gasp paralyzed me in place as her fingers—so cold and slender— brushed along my wrist. Mr. Harris's flesh blackened and disintegrated in my memory. Unsheathing my sword, I aimed to slice my hand off too.

But Cassius grabbed my fist and lifted my arm higher to throw me off balance. "Look, Nora."

Maya remained in place, her body lifted to reach my hand but slumped over with her head down. My skin remained intact. What she always wanted...was to be an Unfortunate.

Maya's head slowly lifted. Hope poured out of her eyes like rain. "I can finally reach you."

Heat rose until my blood boiled, and my fear twisted into anger. I detached from her touch. My deafening slap darkened her cheek.

She held her face in shock as tears swelled in both our eyes.

"You *did* reach me," I corrected. "You had so much respect and admiration from your subjects and staff. And you wasted it when the time actually came for you to lead them. You only thought of yourself. Is this why you ignored my warning?"

My voice then elevated into a yell. "Did you want Cassius to take over this entire time? All of this so you could relive the moment he returned to you? So you could finally become an Unfortunate?!"

Maya quivered and sank lower to the ground. She struggled over her words, "I'm doing what should have happened in the first place. I should have died at the Determination." She inhaled, regaining her strength to say, "But I'm still alive."

When Molly lost her Gift, she needed to remain in the infirmary's care for two weeks before she was considered stable. Maya could still die without the same treatment.

"Nora, please disengage." Cassius spoke in a calm voice. I realized that my sword was still within my grip, ready to strike. AGM soldiers bristled around me. I sheathed my weapon, but I kept my hand on the handle. "She followed my will, so it's done."

"Your will? She trusted you!" I countered and then gestured to the Gifted bodies surrounding us. "Is this *your* will?!"

"Yes." His voice was stern, indisputable. "They follow me and therefore, they follow the Divine."

"Then how can you do this to her? To them?"

"Because I've come for judgement."

All words stiffened from my voice. We were right back at the Determination with him begging me to understand. Surrounded by piling bodies, red armbands, and a defeated sister.

"My people stand by your side because they know it to be true," I whispered his words.

He reached for my hand, but I ripped myself away before he could. His lips faltered into a pained frown.

I tried so hard to change the outcome, but all my efforts led us right back here.

"The further you run from me, the harder it'll be for you to understand." He offered space and began ascending the staircase toward the throne. "But know that everyone serves a purpose in my court whether they follow me or not. Even you."

A wince cut my attention away. Isaac Winters crouched with his hands over his head and eyes closed. He was surrounded by AGM soldiers, but they didn't touch him.

Cassius turned slowly, casually. How could he torture Isaac and talk to me at the same time? He grew stronger in so many ways—his Animus Gift no longer needed his full attention to cast it.

"Mr. Winters needs a little more time to pledge his loyalty to me."

I watched as three AGM members lifted Isaac by his arms and carried him away to a place I didn't know. A place where I might be joining him soon.

Cassius ascended further.

As long as my friends were still out there, I didn't care what happened to me.

"Yes, do you know where your team is?" he halted and

turned. "And where they've taken Prince Henry? I quite wanted that Gift, Nora. Your will denied me of it."

You've taken plenty for yourself already, I thought instead of yelled. My mouth weighed heavy on my face now, sunken into a despondent line.

"I see, so you don't know where. No worries. It'll fall into my hands eventually."

He continued to ascend, but I couldn't raise my neck any higher. Bent, lowered, my head heavied on my shoulders.

Something dark and sinking like an empty, vast ocean or an endless, uninterrupted dreamscape consumed my nerves and burned my chest, stomach, my entire being—filling and draining my spirit all at once.

Even though they were safe from the Diviner, my friends were still far from safety. Did they make it? What if they were fighting the AGM right now? What if the AGM were ordered to kill Gifteds instead of capture? My mind scrambled with the what-ifs and then dulled like my very mind shut down.

Red danced along my vision. All around me were Unfortunates who pledged their loyalty to their Divine-chosen king. So why was I still fighting if it didn't matter?

In front of his throne, Cassius gazed out at the ballroom. "We're finally here," he marveled. "So tell me, are you ready to pledge your loyalty to me Nor—?"

The dark blue coloring of the world settled into my heart. The reality of my situation darkened. I was foolish to think that I could make a difference in this world by myself. I was foolish to think that anything I did to prevent the kingdom's unravel was in my control or in my hands alone.

His smile fell.

His expression shifted to disbelief. "What?"

Fixated on the floor, I heard his footsteps charge toward

me. I remained unmoving as his arms clung onto my shoulders. His hand moved to my face, holding my chin so I could meet his eyes.

So much panic and worry and heartache starred that night sky. Was it the same sky I fell from when I was downcasted?

"Where is it?" he demanded. "Where is your light?"

I couldn't muster enough energy to squint, to show him my confusion. My face remained the same. He twisted further into despair.

"What happened to my brightest Unfortunate?"

Epilogue

"Fern!"

I turned, startled by my name.

"What Kai?"

"Are you sure they won't be able to get in?"

I finished sealing the hole I dug out, trapping us underground. Flexing my fingers, the ground hardened above us in case any Anti-Gifted rebels stood over our hiding place. Their feet scattered along the ground like rats, running from all angles.

"I can always...just add more dirt." A large inhale finished my sentence as I fell onto my butt. Outstretched, my arms touched other people, so I quickly nestled into my own space. From the strain in my arms, making more room for the others would be wasted energy.

Leo lit a flame in his palm so everyone could see each other.

"How long will we have air with that?" Skylar asked, her body pressed closest to the wall.

"Hard to say without an exact measurement of the space." Kai examined my work. "An hour or two at most."

"That doesn't give us long," Skylar warned with her usual pessimism.

"It's enough to keep us alive now. That's what matters." Leo hovered over his sister. "How are you doing?"

Persephone adjusted to place less weight on the gash along her right arm. Leo reached out for Prince Henry, but she pushed him tighter against her chest. "I'm warming him."

"Let me do that," Leo offered. "I'm a Mati too."

Persephone glanced at his burnt arm. "Don't give me that right now. Give yourself more time to control yourself. Prince Henry is too important."

He pouted.

"Hey," his sister urged, "at least we'll both have scars on our right arms. Back to being twins."

Leo scoffed and rolled his eyes as Kai came over to examine the wound. He nodded along but his expression remained pouted. "Back to being twins."

I stood up in time for Skylar to notice and yell at me. "Why are we hiding from Unfortunates?"

Fiddling with the earth around us, I created a ledge to sit on so I could sit up and see everyone clearly.

Skylar noticed Persephone lying at a weird angle and lowered her voice. "What happened?"

"Sliced while we were ambushed," Leo explained.

Kai gritted his teeth as Persephone's blood marked his hand. "It's long but it's not deep. Just needs a cleaning."

The Mare took the water from his satchel and washed it over her wound in a cycling motion, imitating a river's flow. The water darkened into a reddish-brown color, then Kai dampened the dirt at the other end of the hideout.

Everyone fell silent.

"The city is overrun." Molly looked down at her branded hand. "Our worse fears are coming true. Do you think...Nora is okay?"

My back bristled at the sound of your name. No one responded.

I let go. You were in my hands until you weren't. We were connected until we weren't.

"She's with her boyfriend," retorted Skylar. "She'll be fine."

"How can you say that?" Molly raised her voice. "She saved much more than your life. You owe her a lot, *Stanton*."

Skylar's nose wrinkled. "You don't get to throw that in my face, *Montgomery*. Or do you have a last name anymore now that you're an Unfortunate?"

The two girls wanted to stand but there simply wasn't enough room, and I wasn't going to provide the space for them to fight.

Protect each other.

"Enough!" I yelled. "If you two can't behave as a team right now, I will hold you both under the ground."

"Oh, are you the leader now?" Skylar placed her hands on her hips. "Who decided that?"

Keeping direct eye contact with Skylar, I commanded the

earth to connect with my foot. The dirt loosened, sank, and buried her to her torso within a matter of seconds. The Aura tried to wrestle against the foundation, but I flexed my fingers closer to a fist and the dirt hardened.

I tried reasoning. "Skylar, you know that if you attacked, Cassius would have taken your Gift and none of us would even be here right now."

"Let me out!" The Aura thrashed but was unable to use the stagnant air.

"You'll be let out when you *calm down*. We need to be a team now more than ever. Can I count on you?"

Skylar thrashed less and less.

"Let her out," Leo cut in. "She'll behave."

I looked at Leo, startled that *he* was the one to tell me to stop. After several seconds, I listened and slammed my foot back down. The dirt returned to its original state, and I watched Leo help Skylar crawl her way out of the sinkhole.

She pressed herself closer to the wall again.

"What are you contemplating?" Kai asked me. "Should we go back for her?"

He always seemed to know what I was thinking. I shook my head despite my very desire to do the opposite. There was no way for us to sneak back into the castle without getting caught. My usual optimism was removed from my voice.

"No. I'm thinking about what Nora told me right before she...let go."

Protect all you can: Gifteds and Unfortunates.

How were we meant to do that? We couldn't even manage to bring Gifteds and Unfortunates together when the Diviner taking over was a threat rather than a reality.

"She made me promise," I noted.

Molly tilted her head. "What kind of promise?"

Sighing, I thought of how expansive Iridion was and how small I was in comparison, thinking of how daunting my goal was and when we danced in a field of unity flowers. The world became so small when we had each other...perhaps there was hope for us yet.

I could already see the map of Iridion take shape along the dirt wall in front of us as it formed in my mind. We looked at its indention.

"An impossible promise," I replied. "One that I can't do alone."

Acknowledgments

Publishing means nothing without readership. You brought my dreams into reality, and I couldn't finish the second installment without each and every one of you.

To our Divine, I thank you for all you've given me in both life and spirit.

To Joel Seymour and his family for loving me well.

To my family for pushing past doubt and continuously supporting me. To Isaac Cook for keeping me humble and to Michel Way for inspiring Chapter Twelve.

Thank you to all other writers within the community who shaped *UNRAVEL*:

To Claerie Kavanaugh for being my development editor and helping me shape and challenge my characters.

To Whitney McGruder for being my revising editor in Book 1, my copyeditor in Book 2, and making me a better overall writer.

To Catherine Downen for assisting with the book layout and offering advice and assistance within the self-publishing world.

And a shout out to Haley Newlin for encouraging me to

publish in the first place well before I even knew her.

Thank you to all my lovely artists:

To Darian Ray for creating my character stickers and being a great friend.

To Bojana Gigovska for bringing my chapter and cover illustrations to life.

To Milan Krstevski for creating beautiful full cover jackets and being patient with me.

And a shout out to Katelynn Schmidt for sketching out the Galdor Academy crest over the summer of 2021 that became *Unfortunate*'s cover.

Thank you to my dedicated Author's Community on Discord:

Joel Seymour, Katelynn Schmidt, Morgan Ferqueron, Mei Scot, Isaac Cook, Rita Rose, Catie McKee, TFlexSoom, Lauren Krechel, Tyler Yancey, Aunt Joyce, Ryan Thompson, Darian Ray, Michaela Clancey, Makoto Booth, Ethan Yamashita, Devon Haynes, Brooke Tipton, Kim Seymour, Kimberly Weaver, Aimee Robinson, Kelsey Wise, Johnna Internicola and her brother, Stephen Walters, Macie Johnson, Emily Craig, Johnelle Weekley, Rebekah Wanner, Uncle Dave Seymour, AHeckin'Mess, emma, and Mozelle Jordan.

Thank you to those who pre-ordered UNRAVEL during its take #2:

Joel Seymour, Morgan Ferqueron, Johnna Internicola, Arielle Wilder, Emily Craig, Vanessa Lozano Enriquez, Whitney McGruder, Aimee Robinson, Joyce Cavignac, Lauren Talley, Mei Scot, Michel Way, Lauren Krechel, Chaz Giles, Kim Seymour, Stephen Walters, Tristan Hilbert, Hanan Taylor, Makoto Booth, Angelina Vita, Rita Rose, Emilia

Ferreyra, Brooke Tipton, Lauryn Fenwick, Tyler Yancey, Catie McKee, Claudette Seymour, Debbie Seymour, Mark Seymour, Neil Myers, William Wilder, Brenda Wilder, Lillian Craton, Isaac Cook, Lindsay Seymour, Zac Seymour, Katelynn Schmidt, Andrea Bowers, Anna Connelly, and Jordan White.

A special appreciation to Kaitlin Skawinski for giving me a place to stay while revising this novel. To all the flames and waning waxes from late night writing, I thank you for your warmth and sacrifice. To my planner for keeping me on schedule. To all the coffee shops for adding to my aesthetic. To the Heathers Musical for channeling my antagonist, and to The Head & the Heart for keeping me company. And to my laptop for five marvelous years—you were by my side day in and day out.

Appendix

GIFTS

Animus: Ability to be with you.

Examples: Prince Cassius Iridion, Prince Henry Iridion

Aura: Ability to manipulate and control you.

Examples: ~~King Daltus Iridion~~, Mr. Stanton, Mrs. Stanton, Skylar Stanton, ~~Cal Hilfrey~~, Prince Cassius Iridion

Avlis (Ah-v-ILL-ss): Ability to manipulate and control you.

Examples: Fern Fairaway, Ms. Daphne Fairaway, Prince Cassius Iridion

Fera (F-AIR-a): Ability to read emotions and speak to you.

Examples: ~~Mr. Peter Harris~~, Prince Cassius Iridion

Imitation: Ability to gain you.

Examples: Mr. Malcolm Montgomery, ~~Molly Montgomery~~, Prince Cassius Iridion

Lux: Ability to see you in the dark. Night vision.

Examples: Minister Gabriel, Mrs. Martha Montgomery, Melanie Montgomery, Prince Cassius Iridion

Makan (M-ah-kin): The most powerful Gift they underestimated.

Examples: Prince Cassius (Ka-see-uhs) Iridion, Delilah Fairaway

Mare: Ability to manipulate and control you.

Examples: Isaac Winters, Kai Lancer, Prince Cassius Iridion

Mati (M-ah-t-ee): Ability to manipulate and control you.

Examples: Leo, Persephone, Prince Cassius Iridion

Mute: Ability to shape-shift into you.

Examples: Ebony Nique, Prince Cassius Iridion

Nox: She can never reach you.

Examples: Princess Maya Iridion, Prince Cassius Iridion